Four Brooding Birds

Byron James-Adams

FOUR BROODING BIRDS

Four Brooding Birds
Copyright @ 2024 James Byron Books
www.jamesbyronbooks.com

ISBN
978-0-9756684-9-8 (eBook)
978-0-9756684-8-1 (Paperback)

This story is fictitious. Some long-standing institutions, agencies, and public offices do exist. The characters and situations involved are wholly imaginary, and resemblance to natural persons, living or dead, or actual events is purely coincidental.

Again a big thanks to my Beta readers:
Vic, Mel, Lil & M.D.M.
Cover Art: Canva by author.
Internal Book Design: Ingram Sparks.

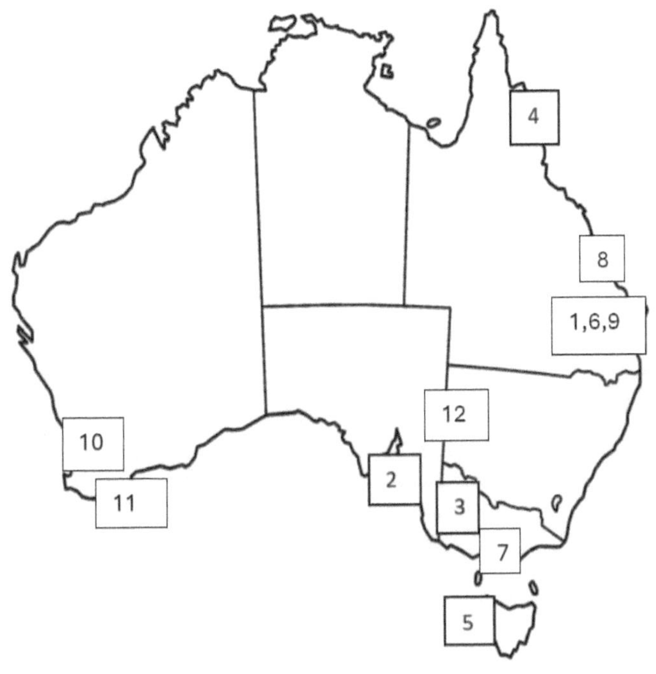

1. Brisbane (Book 1) – One Tricked Phoney
2. Adelaide (Book 1)
3. Pinnaroo (Book 1)
4. Port Douglas (Book 2) – Two Hurtled Gloves
5. Corrina (Book 2)
6. Brisbane (Book 2)
7. Melbourne (Book 3) – Three French Bens
8. Rockhampton (Book 3)
9. Brisbane (Book 3)
10. Busselton (Book 4) - Four Brooding Birds
11. Margaret River (Book 4)
12. Boolcoomatta Reserve (Book 4)

CHAPTER 1

Rosemary Palmer was surrounded by bird droppings, known as 'guano' for the less informed. Rose was a volunteer at the Greater Animal Life Zoo just outside Cairns, Far North Queensland.

Nic Thorn, her business partner and friend, had promised her no more crappy jobs, but she too, had been less informed.

With a shovel in one hand and her face mask in the other, Rose wiped her brow, stretched, and called out to her BFF, Sandy Fraser, who was taking the latest full wheelbarrow away.

'What a crap job, Sandy.'

Sandy stopped and looked back. 'Nic lied to us.'

Rose put the shovel down onto the pile. 'He promised he'd whisk us away on an all-expense paid overseas trip to investigate the latest scam, fraud, or whatever we do, but now has us shovelling bird poo.'

Sandy nodded. 'It could be worse as I was talking to one of the other volunteers this morning, and it's her roster this week to attend to the hippo enclosure. Hippos mark their territory by flicking their scat around, and when they start twirling their tails around like a fan, it sprays everywhere.'

Rose smiled: 'Thanks for the tip. By the way, have you seen Nic? He said something about looking into budgie smugglers. I've been reading up on it. A group of people get their kicks by catching Australian reptiles and birds, stuffing them in cooking pots or plastic tubes, and shipping them overseas. The Department of Agriculture and Fisheries has brought us in to check it all out, and speaking of checking things out, here he comes.'

Nic ambled up dressed in the dark blue uniform of the Australian Border Police and Rose couldn't help but notice. 'Wow, so whilst we are shovelling birdsh you get all prettied up and handsome, dressed as Major Catastrophe.'

'Now that's not fair, guys. Someone has to be a Chief, and someone has to be an Indian, you know, the poop. Oops, sorry guys, wrong choice of words.'

Sandy hadn't yet moved with the wheelbarrow and shook her head. 'This job stinks, Nic. You keep teasing us about going overseas, but so far, you've only taken us to Adelaide, Hobart, and Melbourne, and now you have us shovelling birdsh up here in Cairns.'

'Well, it's for real this time, Sandy, so keep practising. The Border Police have called in Nic Thorn and Associates to deal with the nasties of Fauna smuggling.'

Sandy nodded. 'So, what has it to do with us, dealing with all of this?'

'Well, it's reptile and bird breeding season, and these smugglers don't care if the animals survive. They want the money pot at the end of it all.'

Rose shook her head. 'That's horrible. Does it all leave from here, or is it just a game of snakes and ladders?'

'Not sure yet, but generally it's anything small enough to get into a plastic tube or a suitcase. This is the final stop before leaving Australia. The little critters are collected somewhere else and shipped here. That's why we've been working here, waiting for something to happen.'

Sandy grinned. 'What about the budgie smugglers? I thought one of our ex-prime Ministers wore them on his local beach during summer.'

Nic laughed. 'Thanks for that vision again, it's like an earworm dressed in skimpy men's red bathers.'

Rose nodded. 'Tell us more. Oh, great sensei. Why *are* we here, and how soon can we get into our swimsuits and head for a sunny beach somewhere overseas?'

Nic continued: 'Well, we might have to be settled up here for a while. The spec I've been given has the reptiles and snakes being smuggled by one group, and the native birds by another. They are being delivered somewhere overseas, maybe directly to China, so it may only be a quick trip, depending on if we're following them incognito or it's for a full-blown arrest.'

Rose nodded. 'So, how are you going to be in disguise? You're already dressed as a border Policeman.'

'Good point.'

Nic's phone rang, and he moved away to take the call. 'Yep, we are free. What's happened?' Nic looked at Rose and Sandy and nodded at them. 'Yes, three tickets, and we can do Economy Class.' The call was disconnected, but they had been listening in. 'I have some good news and some bad news. Who wants what?'

Sandy piped up first. 'Well, I'll take the bad news. Rose can have the good news.'

'OK, the bad news is we're not off overseas yet.'

Rose quickly quipped back. 'You promised, and you changed us to Economy Class. We heard you.'

Nic added. 'Yep, well, that's more bad news. We're going west, not north.'

Rose added. 'That's not in the direction of Fiji or Hawaii. So, what's the good news?'

'You can stop shovelling.'

'Damn you, Nic.'

Nic grinned. 'Anyway, that call was from my contact at Curtin University in Perth, Western Australia. A woman was picked up in Cairns airport with her clothes stuffed with blue tongue lizards, and they've tracked to where the reptiles originated.'

Rose looked at him. 'Did she have them wrapped up in her suitcase?'

'No, she was a 'reptile mule' wearing a lizard singlet. They sew pockets into the material and stuff the lizards in them. The little critters were lucky this time, as it's only a five-hour flight from Perth to Cairns. Some survived and some didn't as she had fifteen on her and eleven survived.'

Rose shook her head. 'That's so depressing. Do they get much money if they're successful in getting them through the borders?'

Nic nodded 'One single shingle back stumpy tail lizard recently sold for five grand in China. Wow, that's hard to say, anyway, they only need to get a couple of lizards through, and they're in the money.'

'Surely, there must be a large fine or jail time for smuggling?'

'Yep, big fines if you get caught. My best guess for this woman is a slap on the dewclaw, and she probably won't do any jail time either.'

'So, what's the incentive for them to stop?'

'Only us. In a few days, we're heading to Busselton, Western Australia, to track down where she collected the reptiles. There's a lizard guy we need to meet. He's a breeder, and allegedly, someone broke into his place and took most of his reptiles. You could say he's a bit snaky about it.'

A small flock of geese was now wandering towards them, wondering what all the fuss was about. Nic took a step backwards. 'Have either of you wrangled geese before?'

Sandy shook her head. 'Nope, but I used to listen to the 'Flock of Seagulls,' does that count?'

Nic took another step back and shook his head. 'I don't think so.'

The flock headed straight towards him, and he tried to hide behind Rose. 'Stop hiding, Nic. They only want to say hello. Besides, you've always said a bird in the hand....'

Nic stepped back further. 'No, I haven't. They say animals are attracted to those who don't like them, and I never knew geese hankered for me until I had a little incident with one when I was a kid. It attacked me, and I made it angrier when I threw my shoes at it.'

Rose grinned. 'Wow, our big brave Superman, Nic Thorn, has a weakness. I thought it was kryptonite, but who knew? I would've thought it was something more than an old bird with an attitude problem.'

'I know, right, but they all have those beady eyes. They all want revenge, have long memories, and long necks.'

Rose leaned down to the front bird, gathered it up, and started stroking it. 'Come on, it's just a large white chicken. I'll pick one up so you can cuddle it.' Nic cautiously moved towards it, and Rose added: 'That's not so bad, is it?'

The bird then wriggled in Rose's hands, thrust out its beak, and struck Nic on the top of his head. Rose dropped it softly to the ground, where it proceeded to peck at Nic's leg and he tried to push the bird away. 'You did that on purpose.'

Rose and Sandy began to laugh, and a crowd of tourists gathered around to watch the big blue Border Policeman do his little goosy avoidance dance. Most of them had cameras and phones aimed at him. Nic stopped dancing and bowed.

'Yep, it's true. I am not Superman.'

A few days later, they said their goodbyes to the Greater Animal Life Zoo team, and Nic left a sizeable donation to their cause. Rose, Sandy and Nic were waiting in the QANTAS Lounge at Cairns airport for the announcement of the flight to Perth. Rose leaned forward. 'I saw the receipt for the donation. What did you leave them? Five hundred or so?'

Nic smiled. 'Not quite, maybe with another fat lazy zero at the end. You know how much a zero looks like a goose egg to me, how could I resist? By the way, it was the bonus I was planning to give to both of you for spending the last two weeks shovelling poo. Hope you don't mind.'

'That's OK as Sandy and I have been bumped up to Business Class for this flight, so it'll be champagne and truffles for us. Hope *you* don't mind?'

'Did you use my Business Credit Card?'

Rose nodded. 'Of course, but think about the Frequent Flyer Points we've just earned you, and it was a triple point upgrade. There is bad news though, as only the two seats were available.'

QF712 for Perth, now boarding.

They moved to the gate where Rose and Sandy took great delight in pointing out to the steward that Nic's seat allocation was at the back, way down the back, with all the unaccompanied children.

After being provided with a glass of chardonnay, Rose and Sandy were comfortable and began to watch the inflight safety instructions.

The captain came out from the cockpit, manoeuvred around the flight attendants and moved up to them: 'Hello, I am Captain James T. Kirk. I believe you two are joining us on the Enterprise Tour to Perth. I have been asked to welcome you aboard. Hope you enjoy the flight.'

Sandy looked at him. 'Are you one of Nic Thorn's mates then Captain James T Kirk? I assume Spock and Scotty are here on board somewhere? Are we being beamed to Perth instead?'

Rose shook the Captain's hand. 'I'm sorry, Captain Kirk. My friend is a little sceptical about names and thinks everything is a set up by our friend, Nic Thorn.'

The pilot rubbed his chin thoughtfully. 'I don't know a Nic Thorn. I once got pricked by a rose thorn, is he any relation?'

The flight steward standing next to the Flight Captain stifled a laugh. Rose stood up. 'Damn you, Nic. Where are you?'

'I'm sitting behind you.'

Sandy interjected. 'Hey, that's not fair. We paid good money for these tickets to keep us from the riffraff, and you're now sitting behind us. I hope the seat next to you has a snivelling child.'

Nic responded: 'Nope, there's no one, and I have both seats.'

Nic then stepped into the aisle to shake the Captain's hand. 'Heya Phil, it's been a while. It's good to see you're still pushing tin across Australia... How are Kathy and the kids?'

'Everything is great, mate. Perth is now home. We bought a place in Cottesloe a year or two back when the mining boom stopped being so crazy. On a good a day, we can see over to Rottnest Island.'

'You always said flying was in your blood, and you'd be a commercial pilot when your Australian Air Force stint was over.'

The Captain nodded. 'Hey, I'd better fly this thing before the passengers wonder why I'm out here talking to you, and not in there talking to them. Sorry, but I can't let you take control of this one. It doesn't have a parachute in the tail like the little rattlers you tend to fly.'

The Captain returned to the cockpit, and the flight steward moved away in readiness for take-off, and he made his announcement:

'Good morning, ladies and gentlemen. I am Captain Phil Goldberg. I have Co-Captain Stephanie Winton with me. The flight time to Perth is around five hours, and for the two passengers seated in

Business Class seats 4A and 4B, you will arrive half an hour earlier. To infinity and beyond.'

After reaching flight altitude, Nic leaned towards Rose and Sandy and passed through a portfolio. 'This is the brief on the reptile investigation. Have a read, and let me know if there's anything you want to talk about. I'm going to get some shut-eye. I'm sitting all alone, so I won't get my shoulders dribbled as I often do when sitting in the middle between you two.'

Rose leaned around the arm of the chair. 'You want to bet?'

CHAPTER 2

They landed in Perth, collected the luggage, and moved towards the Car Rental booths, but the one they were standing in front of was unattended.

Sandy noticed the absence of the receptionist. 'What, no driver this time? We had 'Driver' in Adelaide and then his brother 'Driver Two' in sunny, rainy, windy Melbourne. Is there nothing left in the budget?'

Nic called out 'cooee', and a young man appeared below the desk. 'This is our driver, BB.' He was dressed in a dark green khaki safari suit, and the cap on his head read: Australia Zoo Beerwah.

They knew the twenty-year-old from Tasmania as he'd helped them close down a scam involving an alleged Thylacine sighting.

Nic and BB shook hands, then BB hugged Rose and Sandy.

'Thanks for letting me be your driver. Nic asked me to find a suitable vehicle and I couldn't go past 'Gladys' as she's a sixty-year-old Kombi but drives like a bomb. It has three bench seats and plenty of room for other stuff.'

They moved outside, put the luggage into the car, and headed towards Busselton.

Rose leaned forward. 'Have there been any more sightings of the elusive Tassie Tiger?'

BB grinned. 'Nope, but did they like to catch up with Griff and his crew?'

Nic shook his head. 'Not yet, and thanks for making yourself available for this investigation. I needed an animal expert, and you were the first person I thought of who could join us at such short notice.'

BB smiled. 'So where to? Where are we staying?'

'At the Ithaca Motel, in Adelaide Street. It's a little downmarket compared to what Rose and Sandy prefer, but we are on a study trip anyway.'

Rose piped up. 'Happy families? BB was not mentioned in the brief, so how will that work?'

Nic continued. 'As per the brief, you two are Uni students doing your final thesis, and I'm your private tutor, and now BB has joined us from Tasmania to complete his scholarship. It might not come to that as I'm keeping this one as simple as possible.'

BB nodded. 'Thanks, Nic, I've always wanted to go on a school excursion.'

Sandy laughed. 'Just when did you leave school?'

'I'm still doing my last year of high school, although I'm like nearly twenty. The Tassie wilderness is my outdoor school. My parents recently got divorced, left Penguin and dropped five thousand in my bank account. They told me to make my way in the world, like around Tasmania anyway. This is my first adventure over the ditch onto the big island.'

Rose continued. 'Wow, that's many changes in six months. What about the guide job at Cradle Mountain that Nic set you up with?'

'It's too cold there now, and I like the weather too unpredictable, but I kept in touch with Nic, and he offered me this gig.'

'You know he doesn't pay wages, don't you?'

BB shrugged. 'I don't need no credit card to ride this train.'

BB raised his eyes in the rear-vision mirror. 'Rose, that's a line from "The Power of Love" by Huey Lewis and the News. It's a great song, and a great film too. Michael J Fox – "Back to the Future."'

Nic sighed. 'If I only had a DeLorean, I could travel back in time and find myself, but, my life doesn't need the added complication of alternate timelines. I'm already confused about living in this one.'

Rose shook her head. 'Anyway, tell us more about this investigation.'

Nic continued: 'The breeder we are meeting in a few days has recently lost most of his reptile stock. He also said they must have drugged his guard dogs.'

BB nodded. 'Does he have a zoo or something?' Nic added. 'He's a breeder for the zoos, and told me it would take years to get his stock levels back up.'

They were now driving along Adelaide Street, Busselton, and BB pointed towards a hotel.

'Hey, this looks like the place, Ithaca Motel, and we're only a short walk to the jetty, then it's a long, long way to the end of the jetty and back. It takes like about an hour for the three-kilometre return trek. Well worth it, but there's nothing but open blue sea at the end.'

Nic nodded. 'No worries, BB. We have a few nights here, and depending on what happens at the reptile place, we might venture into the Margaret River winery area to sample some of the wares.'

They checked into the Hotel. Rose and Sandy were sharing a room, while BB and Nic shared another.

There were two envelopes left for Nic at the reception desk and he assumed they were from the reptile park owner as they had a gecko watermark in the top right corner.

The envelopes contained a note: 'Trust No-one' and the other: 'Belles of St Cl m nt. Add heat.'

The group entered Nic's room with the mail, and he placed them on a table.

Nic found an iron and filled it with water for steam, then began to run the hot iron above the papers. 'It's basic science stuff. There might be another message here written in lemon juice. It needs heat added.'

Rose picked up the envelopes. 'This isn't computer printing. It's from a typewriter. I haven't seen this font for years.'

BB looked at him. 'Why leave the notes?'

Nic added. 'I have no idea. I'm meeting with the reptile guy tomorrow night at Albies Bar and Bistro.'

There was nothing more on either note despite Nic's attempts to raise the supposed secret writing.

Rose unplugged the smouldering iron. 'Well, nothing means nothing until it means something, right?'

Nic nodded. 'True. So, let's go and check out Albies Bistro. It's about a ten-minute drive. BB, would you mind not having anything alcoholic?'

It was around 7 p.m. when they arrived at the bistro. They paid the $10 cover charge, found a table and ordered their meals. A couple of roadies were setting up the sound equipment, which included a Karaoke machine.

One of them folded out an easel: *'Open mike night'*.

Rose knew Nic and BB would likely join in as they did an impromptu performance together during the Tasmanian investigation.

Rose sighed. 'Are you two going to get up then? I'm sure your 'Elvis the Pelvis' routine would go down well here, too.'

Nic looked at the stage. 'Maybe you and I could do Dolly and Kenny's version of 'Islands in the Stream.' It should be fun.'

Sandy added. 'Why not double down? Have BB and me up there, and we do something as a quartet. We could sing "California Dreaming" by The Mamas & The Papas. I'm sure it will be on the list.'

The waiter dropped a form on each table with a list of songs available and an allocated time. 'We'll collect this from you when you get your meals but you don't have to get up if you don't want to. Three songs max, no dirty dancing, swearing, and no rap. This is a respectable joint.'

Nic wrote Sandy's suggestion on the paper but hid his other song choice from the others. The waitress returned, collected the form with their meals and drink orders and smiled at Nic.

'Your songs have been accepted. Good band name, too.'

The waitress moved away again and Rose looked at Nic.

'What've you done? Two songs? Please don't embarrass us.'

Nic smiled. 'You'll know them. One was Sandy's suggestion and the other one you've both sung before.'

It was nearing eight o'clock, and the last group had just come off the stage from singing 'Everly Brothers' covers and they were very good.

The next group stood up. They were was a quartet of family members, and the emcee announced the band name: 'These guys are the Jackson Four. Michael couldn't make it tonight, there was something about his monkey going bananas.'

The group covered two Jackson 5 songs, then a version of 'Country Roads' by John Denver. It went down well with the appreciative crowd.

The MC thanked the previous troupe and nodded to Nic's table.

'Ok, all you Mamas and Papas fans out there tonight, you are in for a treat. These guys have come all the way from the east coast of Oz to perform for you tonight. Please warmly welcome 'The Dusty Spring Fields' with their version of 'California Dreaming,' then they'll hit you with one of Dusty Springfield's classics.'

Rose groaned, Sandy laughed, and Nic nodded. 'Yep, we are doing Wishin' and Hopin,' this time with two grooms.'

BB looked at Rose and Sandy. 'I didn't know you two were singers. How many gigs have you guys done?'

Rose shook her head. 'Just the one at the Rockhampton Show. We used the theatrics from the opening scene of Julia Roberts's film 'My Best Friend's Wedding,' with the theatrics added. Do you know the film?'

BB nodded. 'It's like one of my mother's favourites. I've seen it like ten times.'

Nic stood up. 'BB, you take Sandy as your bride and leave Rose with me, but first, it's the California Dreaming song. Do you know that one too?'

BB nodded again. 'I can do some 'air guitar' during the middle eight.'

Nic smiled. 'Sounds good, BB. Whatever toots your flute.'

Nic's group went to the stage, and he noticed Rose take a large gulp of wine for courage. They waited for the song to start....'*All the leaves are brown....*'

When it got to the pan-flute instrumental part, BB was down on a bent knee doing his best air guitar routine, then he re-joined the group, and the song faded out.

The crowd was up on their feet, cheering.

Once their second song commenced...'*Wishing and hoping and thinking and praying*', Nic collected two spare white napkins from off stage, which Rose and Sandy then shrouded over their heads, and they started with their backs to the audience.

BB and Nic sang the first verse, and Rose and Sandy turned around when the second verse started. The crowd was in rapture.

BB and Nic went down on bent knees as the song ended, lightly holding Rose and Sandy's hands. The song finished, Rose and Sandy slapped the men's hands away, took each other's hands, and sat back down at their table. Nic and BB followed them despondently and sat down.

The crowd cheered for more.

The emcee again stood up and moved to the stage. 'Great act, guys. They told me it was their first time doing the routine. So, unless the next group of singers can outshine them, I think we may have found our winners tonight. Anyhow, here's our next group. They call themselves 'The Monks with Keys."

A trio of men moved from their table, jangling their car keys and waving their hands around, behaving like gorillas. They had chosen two songs by the English band 'The Gorillaz' and then did a version of 'I'm a Believer' by The Monkees.

Meantime, a man approached Nic's table dressed in a black duffle coat, with the hood covering his head. His hands were deep into the coat pockets.

'I'm looking for Thorn.'

Nic stood. 'Yep. That's me. You're early. It's supposed to be tomorrow night.'

'Couldn't wait. Need to talk about me lizards. Not here, go outside. Meet me by da bins.'

Nic nodded, then looked at BB.

'Guys, meet me at the car as we'll be leaving in a tick. I'll be back in a ...um a tick.'

Rose paid the bill and met the others at the Kombi, but Nic wasn't there. They stood and waited, then decided to wait inside the car.

Rose brought up the karaoke result. 'Oh, by the way, we won. The cashier told me that we forfeited the first prize as we weren't supposed to leave until all the votes were tallied up.'

Sandy rubbed her hands together. 'What was the prize, Rose? Fifty dollars?

Rose shook her head. 'It was a meat tray. Not much good for a bunch of vegetarians like us.'

CHAPTER 3

Nic ambled over twenty minutes later and stepped into the Kombi. 'That was Jim Sarfek the reptile man. I was expecting to meet with him tomorrow. He talks a little slowly as he's copped one too many snake bites in the face.'

Sandy nodded. 'And that's exactly why my friend 'Pucker' insists on kissing everyone she meets on the mouth. If she gets one more Ice Hockey puck through her face grill, it's no more smooching for her. I don't know if a puck in the moosh would be worse than a snake bite.'

BB laughed. 'Nic's told me about her. If I am ever in Brisbane and have the pleasure of meeting her, I like must remember I have a bad cold.'

They returned to the motel and were now in Nic's room. BB opened the conversation. 'What else did you find out from him?'

Nic started making coffee. 'Well, he almost lost everything. Snakes, reptiles, and even his frogs. They were boxed up and gone. He wondered why his guard dogs didn't react and discovered they'd been drugged, but they've since recovered.'

BB sighed. 'How many reptiles?'

'About sixty in total. He told me his record-keeping was a bit slack and I was surprised at that. He's a registered reptile breeder and needs to be audited every six months for safety compliance. He has an audit due in two weeks, but he thinks whoever took his little critters might've known that.'

Rose added. 'Is it a self-audit?'

'Nup. He has to be registered with the Parks and Wildlife Service, and they do the inspection. Jim said if he can't recover his reptiles, he won't recover his business.'

BB nodded. 'When are we heading there?'

'Tomorrow afternoon, to get an idea of how it all went down. The shingle-back lizards, the woman was caught with in Cairns are his. He uses an ultraviolet tattoo system to identify his stock, so those are being returned. Some of them died, but he's hoping he'll still have a mating pair.'

Rose sighed. 'Are Sandy and I still free to do the jetty walk tomorrow?'

Nic nodded. 'Sure. BB and I will have a look at the Margaret River Airport to see if anything is being organised from there. I don't think the reptiles would be leaving via the Perth Airport as it's too risky and busy.'

BB nodded. 'Do we know where the woman in Cairns picked them up, as that would be a start?'

'Yep, but she's not talking. She did say she didn't know she was wearing a singlet full of live lizards.'

Rose shook her head. 'That's stupid. Did someone slip it over her head whilst she wasn't looking?'

Nic grinned. 'Who knows, Rose, but I suppose it's always easier to deny than take the blame. That's the legal system we work with, innocent until proven stupid.'

Sandy nodded this time. 'We'll see you about lunchtime then. Rose and I will do the famous jetty, then hit the famous Busselton shopping precinct. We might even find a famous quokka or two to snuggle and smuggle them back to Brisbane.'

Nic shook his head. 'I don't think so, Sandy.'

Sandy grinned. 'Who said anything about putting the little hoppers in our hand luggage? Have you seen one? They are the happiest little creatures on earth, and nothing would make them happier than sharing a return Business Class ticket seated next to us.'

Nic nodded. 'OK, I tell you what, before we return, I'll see if we can take a hop over to Rottnest Island and visit the quokkas.'

Rose shook her head. 'Can we take the ferry instead? We'll be flying over water, and I don't think having a plane with a parachute in its tail would be any good if we crash into the sea.'

Nic grinned. 'They do make planes that can land on water.'

Rose sighed. 'Well, on that note, we're going to bed, and I'll think about it, so good night from us.'

Nic saluted. 'By the way Sandy, planes have weight restrictions, so you won't be able to bring any quokkas back with you.'

BB then stood up. 'I'll be off to bed now too. Do you know how to get to the guy's reptile farm?'

'Yep. After passing the Margaret River airport, we turn right into Acton Park Road, and then a left onto Fish Road. It's just after the Nature Reserve. We can't miss his farm, apparently.'

'So, it's like near the airport?'

Nic nodded. 'Sort of, and that's why I think it all happens from there. Jetstar flies directly to Melbourne from there, but that's a long way from Cairns. Hopefully, they can get something out of the woman caught with the lizards.'

Rose and Sandy left the room, and BB went to the bathroom to change for bed, so Nic called his computer geek cousin, based in West Brunswick, Melbourne. They'd met up as youths in Mildura and studied together at the University of Brisbane. Chewy had returned to Victoria to set up a cyber investigative service, and they had been working through the capers together ever since.

'Hey Chewy. What are you up to? Oh, sorry mate, I forgot about the time difference. We're in Western Australia. What's the time there?'

'About one a.m. What's up? I'm still up as I'm gaming with someone that's in Sydney. We've got a couple of Russians running for their lives.'

'Just the two of you?'

'Yes, it's two of us against two of them, and they're real Russians too. I think they're in Moscow, but I'm not quite sure. They have no idea where Australia is, and they think we're Austrian, so I keep referencing the Alps.'

'Fair enough. Just be careful.'

'Sure *Dad.* What can I help you with?'

'How are you going with that flight analysis for this smuggling thing? And can you let me know how long the critters can survive stuffed in a bag? Oh, and the flight options, whether leaving from regional airports or direct from Perth.'

Chewy responded. 'Sure. I'll have it for you once these Russians defeat us or they surrender. Give me until the morning to send you the report. Better make it lunchtime, as my mate has just had his castle invaded.'

'Thanks, Chewy.'

'Are Sandy and Rose with you too?'

'Yep, and Billy-Bob Kingsman from Tassie. He's the wildlife guy we met doing the Tassie Tiger thing.'

'I can't wait until you're back in Melbourne so I can work in the field again.'

'Stick to the cyber security stuff, Chewy. Your tendency to attack people with your Star Wars Light Saber doesn't make much of a defence.'

'Funny, Nic. I'll be in touch.'

They disconnected, and Nic climbed into bed.

At breakfast, Nic ran through the schedule for the day. 'We'll see you back around one, and pick you up at Busselton Central. Would you mind getting lunch?'

Rose and Sandy nodded, then they waited for Nic to leave, and began walking along the esplanade. 'Where to now, Rose? There's a train that goes along the jetty so we don't have to walk the four k round trip.'

They stopped outside a kiosk and looked at the extensive Busselton pier disappearing into the bay. Rose nodded. 'Let's get breakfast to go and eat it on the train. I'm still not keen on doing the flight to Rottnest Island.'

Rose and Sandy purchased the tickets, boarded the train and the return trip lasted forty minutes, then walked along Queen Street to the shopping precinct.

After buying some outfits in a swimwear shop, Rose again raised her reluctance about the small plane trip. 'As this chiffon is so light do you think it will make a difference to the plane weight?'

Sandy shook her head. 'I don't think so, but what about seeing the quokkas? Have you ever seen one live?'

Rose shook her head. 'Nope, but I've seen the photos of Chris Hemsworth and Roger Federer with them.'

Sandy grinned. 'Well, when we get airborne, I'll bring up the photo of Chris and the quokka on my phone. You can stare at it for the time we're up in the air.'

'Thanks, that might work. Perhaps we can get a picture of Nic and a quokka to see how they compare.'

Sandy nodded. 'With each other or with Mr Hemsworth?'

Rose grinned. 'Both.'

They ventured around the shopping centre, found a place for another coffee, then Sandy googled for the local eateries: 'There's a place called 'Baked.' We'll get something there for lunch.' They located the shop and ordered rolls, sandwiches, and a couple of chocolate eclairs for dessert.

Around 1 p.m., Rose received a text from Nic, and a couple of minutes later, they were back in the Kombi to head down the Vasse Highway towards the Margaret River airport. Rose leaned forward. 'What did you find out at the airport?'

'Not much, but I've arranged for a visit early tomorrow morning. Chewy filled me in on the life and times of smuggled reptiles. If they get cold, they can go into something called brumation. It's the slowing down of metabolism. The critters can effectively go to sleep and survive for long periods. China doesn't treat the Australian lizards as an endangered species, so if you can get them in there, they're welcomed with open claws, so to speak.'

'So, Australia can ban exporting, but countries like China don't ban importing?'

'Yep. It makes you wonder, doesn't it?'

BB piped up. 'They can get like up to eighteen thousand for a mating pair of lizards. This is one war I like can't see us winning, and we have ninety per cent of unique species here too.'

After a couple of hours, they passed the airport and took the right-hand turn off the highway into Acton Park Road. 'Take a left just after the Fish Road Nature Reserve, BB.' BB made the turn.

'Did Chewy find out how the woman flew from Perth to Cairns with a lizard singlet?'

'Sort of. Chewy made a call to the Investigating Officer in Cairns and pretended that he was me. I hate it when he does that, but he reckons he's known me long enough to know how I speak and what questions to ask.'

Rose called out from the rear seat. 'Sandy and I worked that out just after we met you as you speak in gobble-dee-gook, and idioms.'

Nic responded. 'That's not fair Rose. I thought that you, of all people, understood that of all the people, I needed to understand me, and you guys were the first to understand. Understand?'

BB looked over at him. 'Wow, what was that?'

Sandy interjected. 'That was Nic Thorn "double-gobble-dee-idiom". It's a rare occurrence, like a politician keeping a promise. You have to concentrate on getting what he means, but once you do, everything else Nic says makes sense.'

BB added 'Remind me how long you two have been working with Nic?'

'About a year, but Rose has been a little longer.'

'How much longer have you known him?'

Rose nodded. 'About five hours.'

Nic finally spoke up. 'Guys, you're driving me crazy with this stuff. Have you had a chance to read the background profiles?'

Rose called out from the back seat again. 'Yes, but I hope we don't have to use it. Using stuff from a recent television show lacks imagination, and what's the idea that we're your serfs?'

Nic grinned. 'Well, we've been to Bells Beach in Melbourne, and now we're at Margaret River. We're on a surfing holiday.'

Rose looked at Sandy. 'It actually says we're seneschals not serfs, which is the medieval word for being the people in charge of his serfs. It makes us sound more important.'

Nic continued. 'Yep, I'm using Downton Abbey, but only use it for an emergency, otherwise, we're just here on holiday. Good, we're finally here.'

Nic read the sign on the gate.' Hey, that's a good name for the reptile farm.' It was: "*The Reptile Farm.*" Be careful here, as the guy told me he breeds Death Adders, Taipans, Dugites, and Tiger Snakes, but he should have anti-venom stored on site. Just don't take any risks.'

They drove through the gate and stopped at the front of a brick building. The man Nic had met last night was standing out the front with a cloth bag in one hand and a pronged stick in the other.

BB stopped the Kombi, and Nic wound down his window. There were two dogs at Jim's heels: a hairless Chihuahua and the other a tiny Tenterfield terrier. He nodded at the group. 'Wurrup.'

Sandy whispered. 'Surely those two tiny, weeny things aren't his guard dogs.'

The group climbed out of the car and Nic introduced them. 'This is Sandy, Rose and BB. Thanks for letting us look around, Jim. How long have you been here?'

The man nodded again. 'Bout fifty years. My folks started it off. Then they met their maker and me and my boy took over, about twenty-five year ago.' The man called out. 'Desmond git outere. We've got people.'

A glass door slid open at the front of the building, and a forty-ish-looking man came out. He looked at his father, then at Nic's group. 'Yo.'

The younger man didn't remove his hands from the pockets of his jeans. Nic nodded towards him. 'Does anyone else live here? Can you tell me anything else that might help us look into the missing reptiles?'

'Well, I got an adopted girl. She's in her room. Doesn't like people much. Doesn't help out much with the farm either. Just with the cookin' and cleaning. Desmond's muther, that sheila left us years ago. Bert and Ernie aren't much good either.'

'OK, thanks, Jim. Who are Bert and Ernie?'

'My guard dogs here. These two mutts nipping at my heels.'

Nic looked down at the two little dogs and did his best to keep a straight face. 'So, can you show us where the reptiles were kept? Any idea how they managed to take them away?'

'Sometimes I drink a bit too much, and my boy, he drinks with me. We might've been asleep. The girl, she was up in Perth. Them snakes have been going missing over the last cupla months, but this time, they almost wiped me out. Took the rest of 'em.'

'OK. You told me the snakes are all kept inside, so if my associates walk around the farm, will they get hassled?'

'I'll get my boy to go with them. He's good at killing dem snakes anyways.'

Nic looked at Sandy and Rose. 'One second thought, I'll keep them with me. I'll get BB to walk the farm with Desmond.'

BB moved over to Desmond and held out his hand to shake. 'Call me BB after the king, man. Got to love the blues.' The man didn't react, and his hands remained in his pockets.

Nic then moved towards the entrance of the building and the women followed behind. 'Do you store them in glass boxes or plastic tubs?' The reptile man slid open the glass door. 'No mate, we use dem pits.'

The reptile man slid open the glass door. Paper, boxes, folders, and newspapers were strewn and piled up throughout the room.

Rose whispered to Sandy. 'I wonder if it looked like this before or after they were robbed?' Jim pointed toward the next room:

'Through here.'

They followed the man along a myriad of makeshift aisles and into another larger area. The room contained six hip-height rectangular cement troughs. 'These are me pits.'

Nic walked around the room and peered into each pit. Most were empty, but there were a dozen or so snakes in the last two pits. Jim called out. 'Them are the Addersh and Vipers. Don't reckon you should get too close.'

Rose and Sandy hadn't moved from the door-way, and Rose had a thought. 'Excuse me, Jim. Can I ask a question?' The snake-man looked at Nic, then to Rose, and nodded. 'If ya have to.'

'Where are your kitchen and bedrooms? You don't sleep in here, do you?'

'At the other place, it's down the road a bit. Another building, we sleep there.' Rose called out again: 'Can we go down there? I think we've seen enough here.'

Nic nodded. 'Me too, Jim. Please take us to the other building.'

The man pointed forward. 'We can go out the back door, but you women will need to come past the snake pitch, or we all go back out the front. What ya want to do?'

Sandy called back. 'You two go forwards, and we'll go back this way.'

Jim nodded. 'Works for me.'

Rose and Sandy about faced, went towards the glass sliding door and Rose had another thought 'How old do you think the reptile guy's son is?'

Sandy shook her head. 'I think that's the least of our worries around here.'

They exited the building and waited for Nic to come from the other side so they walked to the corner and saw Nic and Jim standing very still. Nic saw them and called out: 'Stay where you are. It looks like one of the Death Adders is out here.'

Rose and Sandy shuffled back slowly and noticed BB approaching from the other house, but Desmond wasn't with him. Rose called out. 'Stay there, BB. There's an adder loose in the top paddock.'

BB responded. 'Nope, It's all good. Desmond just put it there, it's a pet. He calls it 'Dallas the Dugite.'' It can still kill you though.'

They watched Jim wrangle the snake, and BB jogged up to Rose and Sandy. 'I just met the sister guys. Like wow, and you'll never guess what her name is.'

BB stopped talking as they waited for Jim to put the snake into a cloth bag, and then he took it inside the building. He returned and crossed his arms over his chest.

'So ya met Lucille then BB? She don't like strangers. Just animals, but not me snakes and lizards.'

The group was led through the second building and out the back door, but there was nothing more of interest. Nic nodded at Jim. 'I think we've seen enough.'

Nic's group climbed into the Kombi and waved to Jim, and Nic noticed Desmond was still not around. Nic turned around to face the others. 'I'm thinking something doesn't quite add-er up here.'

CHAPTER 4

Four a.m. the following morning Nic and BB drove to the Margaret River Airport as they were due to meet with Peyton Progil, The Airport Security Manager. The trio were standing on the tarmac waiting for a small plane to taxi to a stop.

The door opened, and a single passenger stepped out flanked by two security staff and Peyton recognised her as the Airport General Manager.

Peyton looked at Nic. 'So, explain why you think this reptile smuggling goes through my airport?'

Nic opened his phone and clicked on an email link showing the woman with the reptile singlet waiting at security screening. She placed her luggage in the tray and stood in the queue.

Peyton was the only security staff member manning the checkpoint, and just as the woman was waved forward, another woman stepped into her space and tried to move through the rectangle.

The alarm sounded on the security screen and Peyton held up her hand indicating that the second woman was to stop, but the woman stepped through anyway.

Nic waited for a reaction from Peyton, but there was none, so he held the screen closer to her. 'Now watch this.'

The reptile woman had slipped through the security screen behind the second woman, just as she had turned around to be re-screened. It was quite well choreographed. Peyton appeared not to notice the reptile woman had stepped through, or she had chosen to ignore her.

Nic heard Peyton take a deep breath. 'Where did you get this? They told me it was missing.'

Nic nodded. 'It was, but my computer guy has access to a few more resources than you.'

A look of concern came over Peyton's face. 'So can you find out who deleted it?'

'Yep.'

'I am the Security Manager, why was I not informed of the security breach?'

Nic shrugged. 'I guess you'll have to ask your boss. She's coming this way.'

The plane passenger approached them. 'You two come with me.'

Nic closed down his phone and they were led into a nearby office. Nic asked BB to wait outside and the trio, along with the two security staff, stepped inside and gathered around a laptop. It was quite squeezy in there.

Peyton crossed her arms over her chest. 'This is my show. What is going on?'

Nic continued: 'Actually Peyton, you've been temporarily relieved of your position pending further investigation. We identified the computer that deleted the file, and unless someone else has your logon, it was done by you.'

Peyton glared at Nic. 'Did someone dob me in?'

Nic smiled. 'It appears that the Whistleblower Policy the government introduced a few years ago has paid dividends, and that's why I'm here so early this morning.'

The Airport Manager and Nic shook hands. 'I can't believe you sorted this out so quickly.'

Nic nodded his head. 'We've only just scratched the surface.'

Peyton looked at both of them. 'What is going on? If you won't let me do my job, how can I work here?'

Nic sighed. 'Just because you delete an email, then remove it from the recycle bin, it doesn't remove it from the computer network. My guy recovered it from the server.'

Peyton stared at Nic. 'You can't do that. It's against our security protocols to allow third parties to access our computer files.'

Nic shrugged, then continued. 'And here's another tip, when you do searches like "How do I permanently remove my emails" or "How much is a mating pair of shingle-back lizards worth," make sure you delete the cookies.'

Peyton again glared at Nic, then sat down and the two security officers stood behind her. Nic then stepped outside and rejoined BB.

'So how did it go in there?'

Nic grinned. 'Well, she sort of confessed. At least we know the how and the when, but she wouldn't say the who, or the why. Oh, and we don't know the where, as there's still the matter of finding a plethora of pythons and the lounge room of lizards.'

Nic and BB then returned to Busselton for a late breakfast, and Nic decided to return to Margaret River Airport to check if the reptiles had been located.

The Airport Manager told him they hadn't started looking for them as yet, and Peyton still wasn't talking. Nic returned to his group. 'They're still looking for the lizards and don't want our help at this stage, so how about I organise a plane for a quick hop to Rottnest Island? It's quokka central over there at the moment.' He walked off singing, *'Those magnificent men in their flying machines.'*

Whilst they were waiting, BB recounted his introduction to Lucille to Rose and Sandy. 'We were talking about Steve Irwin, the animals, all the stuff. Did I tell you her name was like, Lucille? I mean, BB King and Lucille. Lucille was BB King's guitar.'

Sandy leaned forward. 'Sounds like a match made in heaven.'

'And like do you know what else?'

Rose added. 'Tell us more, BB, before you hyperventilate.'

'She had a Tasmanian Devil poster on the wall. Sarcophilus harrisii. It was like right there on the wall. She's the bomb.'

Nic returned and jumped back into the Kombi. 'Did you miss me? I managed to get a plane, so we're off to Rotto tomorrow. We'll spend the day there, then return here for another night of karaoke at Albies Bar.'

Rose shook her head. 'Nope, sorry, I think we've done our dash singing in bars for now, and besides, we might be worn out after an overdose of cute quokka cuddles.'

Nic smiled, and then BB blurted out. 'I've like found a kindred spirit, Nic.'

Rose grinned. 'BB met Lucille. He reckons she's the bomb and has been blown away by her.'

Nic nodded. 'That's the sister, right?'

BB continued. 'But she ain't like any sister I've ever met. She's like from Kenya or Tanzania. There was a flag in her room. It had a red shield on it. She was talking about animal stuff with the brother from another mother. He has no idea and never says anything, and he's creepy.'

'Did you find out anything else?'

'Nope, but she gave me her mobile number. I can give her a call and go back there if you want. Like, I don't need a reason.'

'Good to know BB, and it might be our way back in. Something is going on down there as there's no way he lost those reptiles without inside help. It could be all of them, and I hope Lucille isn't involved for your sake.'

'No way, Nic. She's like a warrior, living with those like two dopes. Man, I'm surprised they like could even get up in the morning, let alone run a reptile breeding business.'

Nic nodded. 'OK, call her back tomorrow and see if we can get back for another visit. I suspect she'll know something about something.'

BB had read about an Animal Farm located at Ludlow, and as it was about a ten-minute drive, convinced the others to spend the afternoon there. It didn't have any quokkas.

CHAPTER 5

As it was now after six, they drove back to the motel and decided to eat in the dining room. Nic had the two envelopes and notes with him, still wondering what they meant.

BB was watching the '90s war movie Memphis Belle on the television.

It went to a commercial break and showed an advertisement for a car yard in Claremont, an inner suburb of Perth. BB looked at the envelopes. 'Nic, the word's spelt wrong. Belle is a girl's name, and Claremont is a suburb of Perth. It's *Belles of St. Claremont.* Not the 'Bells of St Cements.''

BB pulled up his phone and googled 'Belles of St Claremont', but there was no result.

The others soon joined in with their searches, trying different combinations of the words, but nothing was found.

A waitress approached their table. 'Another round?'

Nic nodded. 'Yep, same again thanks, but can you please help us out with something?'

'Sure, if I can.'

'Does *'Belles of St Claremont'* mean anything to you?'

'Oh sure, they're a bunch of fruit pickers based out of Claremont. They don't have a website or anything. It's just word of mouth and operates from a shed in Mrs Herbert's Park. It's a female-only thing. Does that help?'

BB stood up and hugged the waitress. 'Thank you. It does, like heaps.'

Nic watched her walking away. 'You know, in my day, we weren't allowed to hug someone randomly.'

BB looked at him. 'Like, when did you turn sixty?'

Nic looked at this watch. 'Look at that, it's after seven and well past my bedtime.'

The following morning they finished breakfast and BB drove to the beach, not the airport, and parked near the Busselton jetty.

Rose had noticed. 'Hey, this isn't the airport. It's the sea. No wonder you get confused as both are bright and blue out this way.'

Nic nodded. 'I told you we were flying, but taking off from the tarmac is boring as I can use the water for a runway instead.'

A small group was waiting beside a Seaplane tethered to the jetty.

Nic moved towards them. 'Hello, I'm Nic, and I'll be your pilot today. This little plane takes twelve, and there are only nine of us. It's an hour's flight, weather permitting, and as there are no clouds and little wind, we'll have a comfortable flight.'

Introductions were made, and it was established that the other five were from New Zealand.

'This is my friend Rose. Her mother is from Auckland, so she can translate into Long White Cloud language if you miss anything.'

The crowd clapped, and Rose grimaced.

They climbed into their allocated seats, and BB sat beside Nic in the first officer's chair.

Rose was uncomfortable in a small plane, so Sandy located a photo of Chris Hemsworth posing with a quokka.

'The things I do for you.'

Rose nodded. 'That will help, thanks.'

Nic turned to see what they were looking at, so they showed him. 'Hey, I know that guy. I get mistaken for him all the time.'

Nic turned back and began the pre-flight routine, donned the headset and nodded to BB to do the same.

This is MR Charter VH-MOT. Cleared to take off. Busselton Pier.

Nic then turned around to face the passengers.

'I'd run through the safety check, but it's a seaplane. We can't crash land. There's the sea and we're in a plane with floaties underneath. Is everyone good to go?'

There was a murmur of laughter and Nic continued.

'We'll be flying along the coast up to Mandurah, then cross over the Indian Ocean and head for Rottnest Island. I'll have you down near the pier where the tour bus will collect you.'

Nic taxied the plane into the wind, reached take-off speed, and was instantly airborne.

'This is just like driving a car, except no traffic light, and those big grey lumps in the water are whales. I don't want to put us down on one of those.'

They had only been in flight for around ten minutes, and Sandy noticed Rose was already opening her second packet of chewing gum.

'I didn't realise you were such a nervous flyer in these small planes.'

'The flying I can handle, but it's the take-off and landing that I don't like.'

The flight left the land behind, and a little later Nic pointed towards the island emerging in the distance.

'That's Rotto in front of us guys, and, luckily, my co-pilot had spotted it as I was heading for Love Island. Oh, and by the colour of the water, we'll be landing on a sheet of azure glass.'

Nic throttled back and headed down to the landing zone.

The plane gently caressed the top of the water, and he brought it to rest, then taxied to the pier. 'Please stay seated until the seat belt signs have been turned off and the dolphins have moved out of the way.'

The plane was tethered, and the passengers disembarked.

BB called them together and explained that he would be their host on the tour bus.

'I'm actually like from Tasmania, so I'm used to the little black critters that bite and snarl, not like smiling at you with big brown fluffy cheeks. The quokkas like to pose for pictures, so take as many as you like. Please don't touch them, as it's like a three-hundred-dollar fine. They're wild animals and are very precious to all of us.'

Rose looked at Sandy. 'He's good at this animal stuff, isn't he?'

Sandy nodded. 'Yes, he is. Are you going to join the Tour Bus or stay here and have a look at the derelict buildings?'

Rose grinned. 'I'll stay here and walk around the derelict buildings, then have lunch with Nic the Derelict.'

Sandy laughed. 'Me too then.'

They watched the others board the bus, then wander around the buildings and Sandy decided to kneel to take a picture of a quokka.

'What did you find out from Chewy? Did he go all 'Yoda' on you and quote ', *the greatest teacher, failure is...*'

Nic looked down at Sandy. 'Are you talking to me or the quokka?'

'You. I don't think the quokkas would understand me.'

Nic helped Sandy to stand up, and he continued: 'Well after we discovered the inside help at this end, we assumed they would have also known about the security deficiencies in Cairns.'

A group of quokkas began gambolling across the grass heading for the latest group of sightseers, and Rose pointed at them.

'Did you know it's called a shakka?'

Nic nodded. 'What? A pack of tourists taking pictures of quokkas is a shakka?'

'Nope you dope, it's what you call a group of quokkas.'

Nic shrugged. 'I always thought it was called a quoddle. Anyhow, the woman got caught as the Cairns airport was trialling the full-body scanners, randomly taking people from the departure lines. The x-ray showed a few extra bibs and bobs, and besides that, she was wearing a woollen coat. It was thirty-five degrees with eighty per cent humidity.'

Rose nodded. 'I assume she didn't know who put them there?'

Nic grinned. 'Yep, denied it was anything but her body then started to panic. A man came up and tried to help, so they grabbed him too, and as it turned out he was part of it too. He had frogs in his underwear, she'd given them to him mid-flight.'

Rose grinned. 'Instead of wearing boxer shorts, he had boxer frogs.'

'Yep, lucky the frogs weren't poisonous, other-wise, he might have croaked.'

Rose cringed at Nic's response.

'Anyway, enough of that, tell us about this little island we're on. Do you know how long have these quokkas been here?'

'Nup, but a Dutch dude discovered the island in the sixteen hundreds, Willem De Vlamingh, he mistook the quokka for giant rats and that's how it got its name. The island was attached to the mainland until about seven thousand years ago, and it's been a penal colony for looking after penals, a military colony for looking after the military, and an alien camp looking after aliens.'

Sandy shook her head. 'You're making that all up.'

'No, I'm not. The little green man who just served my green tea told me so.'

Rose sighed. 'Nic, you have to put on your serious pants now as you're about to fly us back to Busselton.'

'Who says we're flying back? It's only about eighteen kilometres from the mainland. A good swim on a beautiful day like this, and I've already handed back the keys to the plane.'

Rose added. 'We didn't bring our swimming togs or anything to sleep in.'

'The quokkas won't mind.'

'Nope, but we will. The rooms around here are three stars, and we're five stars.'

Nic nodded. 'Good point. How about we take the ferry back to Perth, then Uber down to Claremont to check out the site the waitress mentioned, and train it home from there? It will take us about four hours to return to Busselton. BB can make his way back if he wants to stay here overnight.'

Rose smiled. 'That sounds like a plan. BB told us this morning that Lucille was going to Perth for a few days, so I assume he'll meet her there and want to come back with us.'

Nic nodded. 'He didn't tell me he had spoken to her.'

'He texted her last night and they started chatting after that. He can't talk about feelings and relationships with you. He needs good advice.'

Meantime, BB and the tour bus had returned to the hotel, and the others joined them at the table. BB was still leading the conversation:

'The quokkas are used to having their photos taken, and that's why they pose. They even have quokka schools around here, and at morning recess, they like playing 'quokka soccer' with a ping-pong ball.'

The small group was hanging on his every word.

Nic smiled and looked at the New Zealanders. 'Sorry guys, he's leading you on as there aren't any quokka schools or games of quokka sokka. Remember, this guy is from Tasmania, and their biggest claim to fame is a Looney Toons cartoon character called 'Taz."

BB nodded. 'Sorry guys. It's just that you're like from over the other ditch, so it's my chance to get one up on you. People from the big island hate Tasmania as they know it's the best state to live in.'

Meals and drinks were ordered, and Nic stood to address the group. 'Another guide will arrive in about thirty minutes to show you around the settlement village and onto your overnight accommodation. I hope you've enjoyed the morning with my team, and enjoy the rest of your stay in WA.'

Nic and his group then moved outside. 'BB, are you staying here for a while or returning with us on the ferry?'

BB nodded. 'I'll come back with you, but I'm going to stay in Perth overnight, then head back to Busselton tomorrow. I'd like to see a bit around the town.'

Nic looked at him. 'Rose told me Lucille was coming to meet you, so I guess you'll have a guide in Perth.'

BB looked at Rose. 'Can't you like keep a secret for at least a day?'

hey boarded the ferry for the ninety-minute return ride and disembarked at the Barracks Street Jetty in Perth where a young woman approached them. 'Hi, BB.'

BB smiled. 'Hi, Lucille. Thanks for coming. This is Nic Thorn, Sandy, and Rose. They were at your place yesterday. We've been over on Rotto. Nic flew us there in a seaplane. He's like the go-to dude and gets called in to look at stuff by all the big kahunas.' Lucille hugged Nic, Sandy, and Rose but didn't move towards BB.

Nic nodded. 'Nice to finally meet you, Lucille. We're heading down to Claremont to look at a place called 'Mrs Herbert's Park.' Do you know of it?'

Lucille handed Nic an envelope and nodded softly. 'I've written down the directions on the envelope for you, so hopefully the Uber driver doesn't give you a round trip.'

Nic noticed it was similar to the one at the Ithaca Motel and put it straight into his pocket without opening it. 'Thanks, Lucille. We'll catch up with you two tomorrow back in Busselton. Look after yourselves, guys.'

CHAPTER 6

They watched the young couple move away and Nic added. 'How did she know to meet us here?' Rose smiled. 'The young'uns need to tell each other everything. Snapchat, Facebook, Instagram, texting, and all that modern stuff. Would you like to see it?'

They huddled around Rose's phone, clicked on BB's profile, and scanned the Rottnest Island photos when she suddenly stopped.

'Hey, what's that? Is that you? Why do you have your shirt off?'

Nic looked at the vision. 'I didn't know he took that.'

'OK, but why do you have your shirt off ?'

'I just wanted to catch some sun. It's not my fault as the quokka's made me do it. Anyway, let's head to Claremont to check out 'The Belles of St Claremont'. The Uber is here, and I never want to see that vision again.'

Rose re-opened the phone and scrolled to the picture. It was gone. 'You deleted it.'

Nic nodded. 'Yep, Chewy finally figured out how to do that.'

Rose looked at him. 'Are you tele-pathetic too? You're nowhere near my phone.'

Nic grinned. 'The programme links into facial recognition software, so if any pictures of me turn up on the internet, they automatically get deleted. How good is that?'

'I took a photo of you when we were in Pinnaroo when we were investigating that bottle recycling thing. Did that one get deleted too?'

'Nup. As long as you haven't uploaded it. I bet it was a nice photo, too.'

They took the thirty-minute Uber ride to Claremont, drove along Victoria Avenue, and down to Mrs Herbert's Park. Nic directed the driver to stop on the side of the road and Rose nodded to the hut on the other side of the park. 'Belles of St Claremont's' was displayed along the fascia board.

The driver called out to Nic as he got out of the car. 'Are you guys going fruit picking? I often bring girls down here, but the picking is women only, mate. They don't let the men near the farms, and your two women don't look the part. Are you just here to collect the boxes?'

Nic turned to face the Uber driver. 'What goes on down here? Why do some women go to the farms, and others collect the boxes? Why aren't they all collected from the farms?'

The Uber driver becomes aggressive in his response. 'Don't go sticking your big nose in here. Sheila won't like it.'

Nic moved away with his palms defensively pointed upwards. 'Whoa, I just want to know where my friends will be working. We're no one.'

The Uber driver moved away and a little further down the road, made a phone call. Sandy was watching the car. 'That was odd as the guy was all friendly, but then went all Hannibal Lecter on you when you mentioned the fruit picking.'

'Yep, it sometimes happens. Sometimes old sheepdogs don't like the new ones.'

Rose nodded. 'What do we do now then?'

'Chewy is doing background checks to find out if there is Council approval to operate a business from here, and also on the business name to find a name behind it. I might need you guys to do some fruit picking. Have either of you done that sort of thing before?'

Rose shook her head. 'No, but think we both know how to pick a good wine and that comes from grapes.'

'Good to know, but it doesn't help. We might have to bring in an outsider. Maybe Lucille could help us, but if not, I might wear a disguise.'

Rose nodded. 'We've only seen your old people's disguises. How are you going to do that as we didn't bring them with us on this trip.'

'Just call me Chris. It might work on a crowd of women fruit pickers who haven't seen a man who looks like me for a while.'

Sandy laughed. 'I don't think so. Even if you had a Thor costume, they'd know you weren't Chris H. He has blonde hair, not brown.'

Rose piped up. 'Seriously, what are we going to do?'

'At the moment, we're going to see if you can get a picking job. Rose, if you play a French backpacker, who has little of the English language, and Sandy, can you play her Russian girlfriend with a bad hangover? I'll play a guy that has no idea of anything. I think I'm good at that.'

Rose and Sandy nodded. 'Touché.' Then Rose added. 'What if the Uber driver has given them the heads up?'

'Play it the same anyway. He didn't hear you guys speak.'

They made their way to the 'Belles' hut, and a rough-looking, red-headed woman in her mid-fifties came barrelling to greet them and was immediately surly.

'Whatcha wants round here, youz trumpies? Ya don't look like any gangers that cud work for me.' Nic was a little taken aback by the woman's aggression. 'I'm sorry, but my two friends have just arrived in Perth and are looking for easy cash from some fruit picking work. I was told this is the place.'

'Who ya bin talking to?'

'I'm sorry, but I can't remember the guy's name,' then Nic had a thought. 'It was Jim Sarfek. He runs 'The Reptile Farm' down in Busselton.'

The woman continued to glare at him, so Nic pressed on. 'My two friends here don't speak much English. Francine only speaks French, and Natarchya is Russian. Do they need to speak English to work for you?'

The woman shook her head. 'I don't care, but won't pay 'em full tote. I'll pay two dollar a bucket. Otherwise, git.'

Nic nodded. 'OK, we'll think about it, can I call you? Or do we return here if they want a job?'

The woman then went very quiet, and Nic wondered what was going on. 'Are you OK?'

The woman again looked at Rose and Sandy. 'I'm thinkin' that's all. I've just lost one of my best gals. Just sent her off to Queensland. If these two can get to da farm in Chittering in da mornin' I'll give 'em two shifts: five to eight. Don't care if they don't turn up. Have they done apricots?'

Nic nodded. 'That's about a three-and-a-half-hour drive. How do they get there?'

'Not my problem. I pay cash only. No banks. Do they have a VISA to work?'

'Nup. Do they need one?'

'Not my problem either. Now git. Ya wasting my time.'

'I'm sorry to hear that, Mrs....I didn't catch your name.'

The woman continued to glare at him. 'Sheila. I'm Sheila. Aint no Mrs, I left that no good fur nothing years ago, and his stupid boy, Desmond.'

Nic then looked at Rose. 'Le Tour Eiffel. Renault, Citroen au fromage.'

Sheila looked at him. 'What's dat ya said to ya chickee-woman? It sounded all Frenchy, and I don't know about that stuff.'

Rose took hold of Sandy's hand, and they turned away and walked off.

Nic followed a few minutes later, and Rose laughed when they arrived back on Victoria Avenue: 'You dope. Is that the best French you could do? The Eiffel Tower and a French car brand served with cheese?'

'I panicked.'

Nic then called for another Uber. 'I think we'll head back to Busselton. Sorry guys, but you've got a job fruit picking in the morning.'

Rose nodded. 'What's with the two shifts - five to eight?'

Sandy took a breath. 'I assume she meant a five o'clock start in the morning for three hours, then we return at five in the evening for another three. It's too hot out here to spend the whole day in the sun picking fruit.'

The Uber arrived, and it was a late-model black Porsche Cayenne. The driver stepped out of the vehicle and assisted Rose and Sandy to enter.

Nic went around to the passenger side. 'I hope you like this as a better mode of transport, rather than the train.'

Rose smiled. 'So, we're not doing the four-hour commute on the little red caboose?'

Nic added. 'Nope, and by the way, this is Elvis the Uber driver, and he can get us back there in two and a half hours instead.'

Rose nodded. 'Thank you, Elvis. It's much appreciated.'

The driver nodded and curled his top lip. 'Mr Nic told me you two wouldn't give me any trouble but said I can drop you off if you don't like my singing.'

They arrived back in Busselton in under two hours and were dropped off at the motel. Nic entered his room and noticed BB wasn't there, so they went into the Dining Room for dinner.

Sandy took a sip of her wine. 'What did you think of Sheila...was she...?'

Nic stopped her from progressing further with her inquiry. 'Not in here. Let's get dessert to go and eat it back in my room.'

The waitress was happy to oblige but was noticeably disappointed when Rose mentioned BB was still in Perth. Nic went off to make a phone call.

While the dessert was being prepared, Rose decided to ask the waitress about The Reptile Farm. 'Hi, Janie. I'm Rose, and this is Sandy. Do you know

Lucille from the Reptile Farm down off Acton Park Road?

Janie smiled. 'Yes. Lucille is one of my sister's friends. There's a group of girls up there from the Rural Clinical School. They're undergrads doing Medicine or Nursing. Once they finish, they look at posting you in rural areas. I didn't think they would want a boy hanging around with them though. He must be something special for Lucille to convince the others to have him join up with them.'

Sandy piped up. 'We spent a week with him in Tasmania, and he has a passion for animals and the environment you can't learn about in schools.'

'Oh, right. I thought he was like your son or something?'

'Sorry, not quite. Rose and I are just thirty, and BB is twenty. We don't think that works somehow.'

Janie nodded. 'What about the old professor dude that you are here with?'

Sandy laughed. 'We'll tell him that, but no, we're here checking out something down on the Reptile Farm.'

'You mean the reptile smuggling thing they're into?'

Rose and Sandy looked at her and were about to ask for more details when Nic returned to the table.

The waitress moved away, and Nic waited for her to get out of earshot. 'OK. I just spoke to BB. He's decided to stay there overnight. He's got the six young ladies wanting to show him the sights of Perth.'

Rose added. 'Seven, if the waitress could go up and join them. Besides, did you see her T-shirt? It's got 'BOSS' on the back of it. A bit young, don't you think?'

'Yep, I saw that and also overheard you ask about the reptile farm. Is there a connection?'

Rose nodded. 'Well, I think we've found another ally, when we mentioned the Reptile Farm, she knew about the animal smuggling that's been going on down there.'

Nic called the waitress over again. 'I'm sorry, Janie, we must return to our rooms for a conference call. Would you mind bringing our desserts to the room?'

Janie nodded. 'Sure, Room 23? It's a slow night so they won't miss me in the restaurant for ten minutes.'

'Thanks.'

The group went back to the room and waited for the dessert delivery. There was a knock on the door as they poured the coffee: 'Room Service delivery.'

Nic opened the door, and Janie was standing there. 'Thanks, Janie, but would you mind telling us what you meant about '*the smuggling thing*' going on at The Reptile Farm?'

The waitress entered the room and continued: 'I'd heard from Lucille that a group of investigators were coming into town to investigate the reptile smuggling. She then sent me a text, and we assumed it was you guys. We then set the envelopes up with the notes, but you guys getting up to speed took a while.'

'Why did you think it was us?'

'Lucille checked with one of her friends who works with QANTAS. You might have met her on the flight, she was the co-pilot, Stephanie. There was a guy called Nic in Business Class. The Captain said something about telling two passengers he was Captain James T. Kirk from Star Trek, and he upgraded him to Business Class.'

Nic nodded and the waitress continued. 'Then I had a chat with BB and knew we'd made the right choice.'

Rose looked at her. 'Sorry Janie, what if we changed motels?

'We got lucky but would've tracked you down anyway. We also had a plan B. Lucille would have cadged a lift with you into Busselton somehow.'

Nic took over. 'That's a lot of planning. It must mean a lot to you to get this sorted out?'

Janie nodded again. 'Yes. Lucille's been trying to work out how to get this all out into the open for years. It's only coming to a head now as the airports are introducing full-body scanners, so they needed to devise another plan to smuggle the reptiles out of Australia.'

'OK, Janie, I didn't know BB had told you anything. He's not supposed to do that. People can get hurt if everything goes south.

'We talked about that too, and he told me what you did with the Tassie Tiger scam. He's so impressed with your cause. What you do is way bigger than this stuff we did.'

'How long did you speak to him? I thought we'd had an early night.'

'About half an hour back and forth.'

Nic nodded. 'Right. So, is he safe in Perth with six chaperones?'

'I'm sure he can handle himself. If you're worried, I can find out where they are staying.'

'I'm not worried, just being careful.'

Sandy interrupted. 'He *is* worried about BB, Janie. He worries every time we investigate these scams and frauds.'

Nic looked at her. 'Sorry, Sandy, please don't go there, as I might have to open my shirt and reveal the Superman symbol on my chest.'

Janie laughed. 'OK then, what do you want to know about the Reptile Farm?'

Nic nodded. 'Nothing at the moment. When are they returning?'

'They'll be home tomorrow afternoon at about two. Why don't you pick up Lucille and run her home as her father would never bother. She catches the bus along Highway 104, and her doped-out brother is supposed to remember to pick her up at the bus stop. She keeps a bicycle at the highway intersection just in case as it's about a four-kilometre ride to the farm. There's a track through the Fish Road Nature Reserve as a short-cut. Is there anything else, I should be getting back.'

'No, and thanks again, Janie.'

Sandy interrupted, 'Sorry, Rose has a question about the age difference between Jim and Desmond.'

Rose hesitated. 'Err, thanks, Sandy ...How old is the father?'

'Fifty-five, I think. We had his fiftieth here about five years ago.'

'And Desmond?'

'Oh, right, he's early forties, so what you're thinking is right. Jim was an early starter. Desmond's Mum left them years ago, even before Jim's folks died. He inherited the farm. You might've met her today if you went to Mrs Herbert's Park. Her name is Sheila.'

Nic nodded and stood up. 'Thanks for all of this, Janie. We'll pick up Lucille and BB tomorrow after-noon and run her home. It'll give us an excuse to return to the farm.'

'Sure, and speaking of things going down, can you please think about what will happen to Lucille if her father and brother get arrested.'

Rose looked at her. 'Nic does that sort of thing too, Janie. My brother and his wife now live in Hawaii. Nic set her up as the resident Golf Pro at Club Wyndham Kona Resort.'

Nic nodded. 'Yep, I did that, but Janie, one last question, if I may? What's with 'BOSS' on your shirt? You don't run the restaurant, do you?'

She laughed, 'No, Mr Thorn. It's *Busselton Old School Scholars*. 'BOSS'.

Nic smiled. 'Again, thanks for all of this, and we'll be in touch.'

The waitress left the room, and Rose looked at Nic. 'So, it had nothing to do with oranges and lemons or The Bells of St Clements. It's funny how we can jump to conclusions about stuff based on nothing, but at least it *was* 'old school'.

'Yep, Rose, so let's remember that for next time. A lesson in that for all of us.'

'But you were the one that reached for the hot iron, then went all Inspector Closeau on us and told us about the secret messages written in lemon juice.'

'That's not true. I grabbed the iron to steam the wrinkles out of my face.'

Sandy looked at him. 'Get out and take the dessert dishes with you then, Iron Man.'

Nic saluted and added. 'I'll see you in the morning, then we'll take a lovely three-hour drive to lovely Chittering Valley. It's all lovely until we get

there, and you two have to hand-pick the apricots
in the hot sun.'

CHAPTER 7

Just after 2:00 a.m., Nic knocked on Rose's door, and they went to the carpark. 'Sorry, we can't take the Porsche this morning as it might look out of place.'

Nic pushed a car fob, and a worse for wear, 2012 Volkswagen Beetle convertible chirped.

'I got this one just for the day. It's called Ringo. He was the best Beatle.'

Rose shook her head. 'Actually, most people believe the magic of The Beatles was they were the sum of all parts. Besides, Porsche and VW merged ten years ago, so technically, it's still a Porsche, disguised as a VW bug.'

Nic looked at her. 'Remind me to wake you up this early every morning. Are you always this perky?'

Rose shrugged. 'Only when I'm about to pick apricots at six in the morning.'

The trio climbed into the car and headed towards the Chittering Valley. It was around three hundred kilometres away.

It was now 5.45 a.m., and the sun was rising. There weren't many other cars, so Nic was able to stop in the carpark outside the apricot farm.

'Remember, you're Francene and only speak French, and Sandy is Natarchya from Russia. Let's hope we don't run into any French or Russians.'

Rose looked at him. 'You know I speak French. Je peux parler fancais.'

Nic smiled. 'Oui. In case you didn't know, that means I know.'

'Actually, it just means 'yes.''

Nic nodded. 'Je sais. I know.'

They were met at the front gate by an angry young English woman who said her name was Thursday and they followed her down a path towards the drying racks. She stopped and turned to Nic. 'No need for any men down here. It keeps things much simpler. You, stay here.'

Nic looked at her. 'My friends don't speak much English. Francene is French, and Natarchya is from Russia. Can I stay and translate for them?'

'No, that's their problem. I'll put the French one with two other French women, Amelie and Dommi. I'm English and I hate the French, so I don't care what they do as long as they do the work.' Thursday then took a breath and looked at Nic.

'Your Russian can stay here and help with the drying. I hate Russians, too.'

'Is Sheila here yet?'

'Nope. It's none of your business when she comes.'

'Sorry, I have another question.'

Thursday shook her head and glared at Nic.

'Sheila told me you could be trouble. What is it then?'

Nic realised he was pushing the boundaries already, so he decided to ask a fruit-related question instead. 'Do you use Sulphur Dioxide on the apricots or sun-dry them?'

'That too, is none of your business. I've had enough of you already. We need to start work.' Thursday pointed at Rose.

'Francene, I'll call you Frankie. You come with me,' then she pointed out the drying racks to Sandy. 'Russia, you stay here and wait for the others to arrive. Ten minutes tops.'

Nic explained to Rose and Sandy what was happening in broken English, and just before he left, leant forward and whispered; 'Be careful, guys, we don't know what this is.'

Thursday left Rose with the two French women, then she headed towards a site shed. It had 'Sheila's Office' painted on the door.

Despite his instructions, Nic decided to stay with Sandy at the drying racks.

Rose meantime approached the two women and held out her hand. 'Je m'appelle Frankie.'

Neither of the women acknowledged her. 'Vous travaillez a quelle heure?'

The elder of the two women came forward, took Rose roughly by the arm and led her a few metres away.

'Cut the crap, Frankie. You're not French, and your friend isn't Russian. I saw you two singing at Albies Bistro, and I saw that man you came with talking to Jim Sarfek. What are you guys up to?'

The woman released her grip and stepped back and Rose realised the woman spoke perfect English so leaned toward the French woman. 'OK. We're here to investigate the underpayment of the fruit pickers in the area and represent the Government of Western Australia. We're about to raid this property.'

The woman grabbed her roughly by the arm again and marched towards the office. 'No, you're not. You're coming with me.'

Rose said nothing more, and when they arrived at the office, Thursday came out to meet them. 'What's going on? I've put Frankie with you two. You're all French, so you should play well together. Just get back to work.'

'Excusez-moi. Cette femme…um…aller aux toilettes.'

Thursday glared at Rose. 'I think that means you need to use the toilet. Already? I'm going to dock her half-hour pay from you for that. Amelie, please show her where they are and be back ASAP. I hate breaking in the new ones.'

Rose nodded and was led by the woman towards the toilet facilities.

Nic saw the commotion and wandered down from where he had been waiting with Sandy.

'What's happened with Francene?'

The French woman looked at Nic. 'You can stop pretending, too. Your jig is up. Wait until Sheila arrives, then the fan will get splattered with the brown stuff.'

'Sorry, madame, I have no idea what you are talking about.'

The woman remained defiant. 'I am not your Madam. My name is Amelie Enqueteurs de Fraude, and I'm not saying anything else until you tell me why you're here. Remember my name, Amelie Enqueteurs de Fraude. Now get out of here.'

Nic took a breath. 'We're just here to pick apricots.'

'No, *I'm* here to pick apricots, so you'd better go before Sheila arrives. I'm telling you to go right now. Return at two o'clock this afternoon, and you'll find out what exactly goes on around here. Now git, and don't forget who I am.'

Nic didn't bother to 'faux' translate the conversation to the others, so they headed back to the Beetle and moments later drove away.

'I think we blew this one, guys, and I hope it doesn't get back to Jim.'

Meantime, Thursday came out of the office and met with Amelie: 'What was that all about?'

Amelie sighed and explained the situation in her best 'Pidgeon English'.

'I told them to git. Sheila told them to come. Get easy money. I told her ...um what Sheila expected of us. Francene cried like a ...petit fille...um... how do you say baby girl? I show her the toilettes, so you wouldn't have to um...be involved. Hope that's um ...OK.'

Thursday nodded. 'All right, I'll let Sheila know when she gets here. I don't like dealing with you French anyway. We still need a replacement for Yoko. Sheila sent her to Cairns, and I think something happened, but she won't tell me.'

Amelie nodded and returned to the orchard to start her work.

Around fifty kilometres away, Nic, Rose and Sandy were almost in Perth when Rose looked up from her phone. 'Enqueteurs de Fraude; of course, Enqueteurs de Fraude.' Is she one of yours, Nic?'

'One of whose?'

'Stop the car when you can. I think we've just been told to be back at Chittering Valley orchard at two o'clock to watch a raid.'

Rose finished confirming the French translation on her phone just as Nic pulled the car to a stop at the nearest service station.

Sandy had been asleep. 'Are we back in Busselton already?'

Rose smiled. 'Nope, sorry, it looks like we're heading back to the Chittering Valley. The French woman, Amelie, told us her surname was Enqueteurs de Fraude. Repeated it twice and told us to remember it. I thought it was an odd surname, so I googled the words. It's French for 'Fraud Investigator'.

Nic nodded. 'Je ne savais pas.'

'You didn't know? So, who is she then?'

'I don't know. I'll get Chewy onto it, but now we're in Perth, we have about six hours to kill.' Rose nodded. 'Let's catch up on some sleep. Can we find a hotel that books by the hour? Oh, that wouldn't look quite right, would it? Forget I mentioned it.'

'Don't worry, I can access a house, even at seven in the morning. You might have to put up with Elvis, though.'

Nic filled up with petrol, rang Elvis, and they stopped in a driveway about twenty minutes later. Elvis ambled out and struck the hip pose.

'You couldn't leave The King behind, could you?'

Rose and Sandy stepped out of the Beetle, and Nic nodded:

'We have to head back to Chittering Valley in about six hours. Have you got a couple of beds for these two?'

'Sure, what about you?'

'I sleep standing up.'

Four hours later, the group was refreshed and Elvis served them coffee. Nic pulled out his phone and read through the last text from Chewy.

'Chewy tells me that Amelie Enqueteurs de Fraude is Emily Walker and is an investigator for

M.I.R.S...that's the Government Agency that looks after wages compliance and stuff here in W.A. Chewy confirmed Sheila's businesses is going to be raided today, both at the orchard and down in Busselton. Who wants to go where?'

Rose looked over to Nic. 'Is Elvis taking the Porsche, or are we still driving the Beetle convertible? I've only just washed the bugs out of my hair.'

Elvis did a little wiggle. 'Ah-ha-hum, I've got access to a helicopter if you'd like to fly.'

Rose shook her head. 'Um...any other options?'

Nic shook his head. 'Well, no.'

'Damn you, Nic.'

'Elvis we can get us there ASAP. How long is the flight to Chittering Valley?'

Elvis grinned. 'It depends on whether we take the scenic route, otherwise, about fifteen minutes.'

Rose continued: 'OK. I guess I can keep my eyes closed for that long, how do we get to the orchard if we fly?'

Nic grinned. 'I've spoken to Emily and it's set up for us to join the raid.'

Around 1 p.m. the group were at Jandakot Airport and had been cleared for take-off. Rose had kept busy googling French expressions and randomly yelling them out at Nic: 'Ah, la vache! Faire l'andouille and En avoir ras le bol.'

Nic finally responded after translating the quip. 'Well, I'm fed up too, so enough of the French stuff, Rose. We're here already.'

Elvis gently put the AS350 Squirrel Helicopter on the tarmac and they joined the others waiting for instructions.

Amelie was the lead and was in the process of addressing her team:

'We've got about a twenty-minute drive to the orchard. I can confirm Sheila is on her way as she has just passed checkpoint Alpha. We'll give her a few minutes to settle, and then we'll come in.'

Amelie then introduced Nic. 'Oh, by the way, this is Nic Thorn and his Associates, and as it turned out, they were investigating Sheila too.'

Nic stepped forward. 'Actually, we're investigating a reptile smuggling racket originating near American River. Sheila is the ex-partner of our main interest, Jim Sarfek. Our information has revealed it may be a crossover.'

Emily nodded. 'Thank you for the update. So, it's agreed, you'll attend, but only as observers.'

Nic coughed to gain Amelie's attention. 'Sorry, but how do you intend to access the orchard? I assume your shift has finished for the day?'

'We're working on that.'

'Can I suggest we use Rose and Sandy? We were there early this morning, and Sheila would likely expect them to still be there even though you told us to leave.'

Amelie thought about the option and nodded. 'OK. Play it that you've come back to look for work again. Don't take any risks, and don't do anything stupid.'

Nic smiled. 'I never do.'

It was nearing two o'clock when Nic, Rose, and Sandy drove back into the orchard, and as expected, Sheila was there.

Nic nodded at her. 'Hello, Sheila. We have returned to work for you. Francene apologises for the confusion this morning, and they are both willing to work for free, just for the experience.'

Sheila glared at him. 'Don't care about what happened dis mornin', I wasn't 'ere. Anyway, I've changed me mind. Can you get ya two girls to do a twirl for me? I wanna look at them proper.'

Nic wondered what was going on but went with it anyway.

He twirled his fingers at Rose and Sandy; they nodded and slowly pirouetted.

Sheila shook her head. 'Giz a look at yar hands, girls.'

Nic held out his own and pointed, so Rose and Sandy held out their palms, and the woman took hold of their fingers with her hands.

'Don't know whatcha tryin to do ere, mate. These girls ain't ere to do no fieldwork as these girls look like they should be in trashy magazines, not in the fields.'

Nic nodded. 'So, my friends can't work for you then? How about my other friends then?'

Nic then put his fingers to his mouth and let out a loud whistle, bringing Amelie and her team into view:

'This is a raid. Everybody stay where you are.'

Sheila glared at Amelie coming down the drive, then Thursday stuck her head out from the office to see what all the commotion was about and decided to make a run for it.

She didn't get very far as she ran directly into Dommi's clenched fist.

'That is from the French. We hate the English.'

Amelie spent the rest of the day going through all the files in the office and confirmed Sheila had been underpaying her gangers for years. The office safe contained several passports and copies of work VISAs. It was assumed she'd been retaining them to ensure the workers would comply with her demands.

Amelie pulled Nic aside and opened the case file that she had been working on.

'This is a good result. Most of the workers were underpaid tourists working illegally. It's a cut-and-dried case. She'll do jail time.'

'What about Thursday? How does she fit into all of this?'

'She was one of the legitimate ones and she did a really good job keeping all the records on the computer. Don't you love the computer-savvy young'uns?'

Nic left Amelie to complete her investigation, collected Rose and Sandy, and Elvis flew them back to Perth.

Rose kept her eyes open this time.

CHAPTER 8

The following day, they collected BB and Lucille from the train station as arranged, and Rose and Sandy attempted a wolf whistle when they saw BB emerge from the oncoming throng.

He was no longer dressed in khaki greens and even his 'Australia Zoo' cap was replaced with a dark grey trilby.

Lucille was at his side, and they were both smiling.

Rose and Sandy helped Lucille load her overnight bag into the Kombi and sat at a nearby table waiting for the others.

Nic took the opportunity to speak with BB, who couldn't wipe the smile off his face. 'I thought it might be tough spending time with them, so we kept telling everyone I was their chaperone. Then I remembered you told me to take it easy.'

BB began to sing the lyrics from the Eagles song "Take it Easy." *Running down the road, trying to loosen my load, I've got seven women on my mind.*

Nic smiled. 'Great song that one. Did you find out anything more from Lucille?'

BB nodded. 'She's like the whole package, Nic, and she's the one that dropped us the clue with the envelopes. It had nothing to do with oranges and lemons, and the bit about adding heat meant she wanted us to give Jim and Desmond a bit of close attention. Would you like to meet up with Janie, too? She's the motel waitress, and her dad has like something to do with Curtin University.'

Nic nodded 'Yep. I hear that you spent the night with them too. How did you manage to keep all that under control?'

'They snuck me into their motel room. The six were sharing adjoining rooms, so I like ducked into the other room if anyone came in. I slept in the bath and showered in the pool area in the morning.' BB then pulled at the front of his shirt. 'They even made me buy clothes as they reckoned I might pong if I put on the khaki greens again. It like cost me about two hundred bucks for all this get-up.'

Nic laughed. 'The clothes maketh the man, BB.'

BB grinned. 'But tell you what, it's like the bomb, man. I like feel different. It's like what we're here for, to meet all the people we get to know in our lives.'

Nic nodded. 'Yep, the stuff I do gets a bit heavy at times, then Rose or Sandy say something, and I find it hard to focus.'

BB smiled. 'Thanks, and...um, if something like goes down at The Reptile Farm, can you help me get Lucille away from there?'

'I can, but that's a big move for her. She's only young and might need her family.'

BB nodded. 'Yes, like I understand, but can you like get Sandy and Rose to chat to her about it then? I don't want it to be coming directly from me. She's looking for a medical residency, and the Regional Hospitals in Tasmania are always looking for trainees.'

Nic put up his hands. 'Whoa, BB, take a breath, mate. That's a big deal for her.'

'I know, but like I've given it some thought, and we've looked at the opportunities for her down in Tasmania. I didn't like to bring it up, but one of the other girls is relocating to Tassie. Her family is re-locating to Launceston with the Grand Chancellor Hotel group. Her Dad is like already there as the Hotel General Manager.'

Nic nodded. 'Well, let's at least get her home then.'

Nic called the group together, and they stepped into the Kombi to head for The Reptile Farm. Nic turned around to face the others.

'We'll be there in about forty minutes. Were you expected back home tonight, Lucille?'

'Yes, but can we try to avoid Jim and Desmond? They're usually drunk by now anyway. I'll be safe if I can get in without them noticing.'

Nic nodded. 'Can I ask you a serious question?'

'Sure, Mr Thorn, but am I allowed to refuse to respond?'

Nic smiled at her response. 'Sure, it's not the Spanish Inquisition.'

'Ah, a Monty Python fan then?'

'Yep, Rose is too, but Sandy has no idea about them, so there'll be no singing of lumberjack songs on the way back please.'

'What's the question then?'

'How long had you planned to shine the sun on the reptile smuggling?'

Lucille nodded. 'OK, that's cutting to the chase. Well, it's been a while. A box was delivered to the farm last year, and it was my birthday. It was wrapped in butterfly paper and everything. I'd thought Jim had finally remembered, but when I ripped the paper off and opened the box, it was full of dead lizards.'

Rose piped up. 'I'm so sorry, Lucille.'

Lucille sighed. 'There was a typed note attached and it read: "*Next time, ensure they survive. I'm not paying for these, nor the next time either.*"

BB leaned over to her and rubbed her knee softly.

Lucille smiled and continued. 'Well, I knew then that it was time I put a stop to it. Sheila was using naïve backpackers as couriers and had an endless supply of them. I feel sorry for Yoko and Kamika as they've just been caught with the smuggling stuff up in Cairns. She had the reptile singlet, and he had the jocks of frogs.'

Nic nodded. 'I already knew about them. They got caught because we got lucky, as it just came down to the full body scanners being trialled at the Cairns airport.'

'Not quite, as a certain young woman in Busselton had the ear of someone at Curtin University.'

BB turned around from his front passenger seat. 'You like dobbed them in?'

'Me? No way. If they found out I did that, I wouldn't be sitting here today, but you'll work out who it was soon enough. This is all ending, and I'll need to keep myself safe. I don't know what resources you have access to Mr Thorn, but have you dealt with this type of thing before? It might get a bit dangerous.'

Nic smiled. 'I've been doing this stuff for a while. Have you got a plan?'

Lucille nodded. 'Yes, I have.'

Nic took a breath. 'I think you best leave to us. We're almost there is there anything else you want to tell us?'

Lucille shrugged. 'I don't think so.'

They drove the rest of the way in silence, turned into the reptile farm and the gate was shut. Jim and Desmond were standing on the inside. BB pulled the Kombi to a stop, and Nic stepped out.

Jim glared at him. 'You git out of the car girl, and git down to your room. I want a little chat with you, Thorn.'

Nic helped Lucille out of the Kombi-van, gave the others a double open-handed 'stay' signal, and walked up to the gate. 'What's up, Jim?'

'My Sheila was on the blower to me yesterday. It turns out she had a couple of visitors at 'Belles', and when told me about em, I knew they were you and ya girls. What ya playing at?'

'Jim, you've got the wrong idea. You invited me here to investigate the loss of your little reptilian sheep and you appointed me as your shepherd to round them up. Nothing more. Have you spoken to her since?'

Jim shook his head. 'Nup. I don't like to, anyway, shush. I'm trying ta think.'

CHAPTER 9

Desmond opened the gate for Lucille she ran down towards the house. BB whispered. 'This is like going all to crap guys. How is Nic going to get out of this one?'

Rose nodded. 'We don't know yet. I once saw him fight an angry dude using only his right thumb.'

They continued to watch Nic for his next move.

'Jim, I can't tell you what to do, but there's no police here. There's me, Rose, Sandy and BB. I don't know what Sheila said to you, but all I was trying to do was to get some fruit-picking work. They're as lazy as, and I wanted to give them a chance at some hard work for once and teach them a lesson. We talked to someone in a pub in Perth, and they told us she was the go-to for ganging. Sorry if we gave you the wrong idea.'

'I think you bullshitting me, Thorn, but you could have brought in the cops straight away. I'll give you twenty-four hours ta find out where my reptiles are, or it's over. So git.'

Nic nodded and turned away, then he noticed that BB was about to get out of the car, so shook his head, and mouthed the word 'No'. Nic stepped into the Kombi and they backed up the drive.

Jim and Desmond hadn't moved.

They drove in silence for a while. BB was staring forward, then turned to Nic. 'Lucille's in trouble. We've got to like get her out.'

Nic sighed. 'I know, BB, but firstly, we have twenty-four hours to shut down his reptile smuggling. It all starts at the Margaret River Airport, just as the grumpy Uber driver sort of told us. Chewy sent me a report, and he's found a link between Sheila's business and a couple of refrigeration units at the airport. The storage units are airconditioned, so the lizards maybe stored there. There are three units in a row. Two are owned by a de-registered Company, Desmond Lou Australia Pty Ltd, and the middle one is supposed to be empty.

BB nodded. 'OK. What did he find out about Jim and the farm?'

'The farm hasn't been lodging the quarterly Business Activity Statements for nine months, so he's getting his money from somewhere, otherwise he couldn't afford to keep the reptiles fed or Lucille at medical school. The Company Search showed Sheila's last name is 'Ball.' She has never married, and her date of birth is 6th August 1965. Desmond's date of birth is 2 March 1978. 'The Reptile Farm' is not a registered business name as Jim operates it under a sole trader Australian Business Number.'

'So, like why the connection to the three units at the Airport?'

Rose was listening in and then realised the link. 'It looks like Nancy Drew and Miss Marple are to the rescue again. I've just worked out a connection. You said Sheila's surname is 'Ball', has red hair, one kid called Desmond, and an adopted daughter called Lucille. If I'm right, I bet she shares the same birthday as that famous redheaded comedienne.'

Sandy piped up. 'Yes, I've just googled it. Lucille Ball's date of birth was 6th August 1911, the same date as Sheila's fifty-four years later. That sounds like a connection. So, let's head to the airport.'

Nic smiled. 'We're already heading there, but thanks for the tip.'

About fifteen minutes later, BB pulled the Kombi-van to a stop by the storage facilities, and Nic went to the office to explain what was happening. The attendant came out with a key ring and a bolt cutter, and they walked along the rows of storage units.

'So, you reckon the Units Eighteen, Nineteen and Twenty are filled with reptiles? News to me, but the lady with Unit Seventeen has been kicking up a stink about a stink. I just thought she wanted a little look-see. Since those American shows have been on TV about us cutting the locks off the units and selling the contents, everyone wants to get in on the act. We only sell the contents of any abandoned unit online. It's not much of a spectacle, but it keeps the storage wanderers out of my place.'

Rose, Sandy and BB were now in tow, and the group arrived at the suspect Unit. The attendant took a sniff of the air. 'You know she's right. These are a bit on the nose, so I hope there's nothing dead in there.' The man then hefted the bolt cutter at the lock and went to pinch the handles together.

Nic warned him. 'You'd better take it slowly as lizards and snakes could be loose there.'

The attendant nodded. 'OK. Hold one of these then, and be ready.' After unclipping fire extinguishers from a nearby wall, the man handed one to Nic and BB, then announced loudly: 'I am the Prince of Eternal and Defender of the Secrets. I have the power.'

Sandy looked at him. 'Hey, you just quoted from He-man and the Masters of the Universe.'

'No, I didn't. This is our special quote from the handbook of the 'Lords of Unit Storages'; besides, the He-man quote would be copyrightable. Under this authority, I can open the units without a police warrant.'

They nodded in agreement, so he cut the bolt and raised the roller door just a fraction. A green snake slithered out from underneath, then a fat green frog followed. Sandy and Rose jumped back. ' I think we've found the right one.'

Nic quickly shut the door before another green snake slithered out. BB grabbed the frog, dropped it into his pocket, and then picked up the two snakes. 'These are Green Tree Snakes guys, like non-venomous. Well, not in Tassie anyway.'

'Good call, BB. I knew it was a good idea to bring you into this investigation.'

The attendant nodded. 'I was going to pick them up, but I'm holding the bolt cutter. If I dropped it, the others may have stormed the door to make an escape.'

Nic nodded. 'I'll get the Parks and Wildlife Service over here to get this place searched.' Nic moved off to make the call.

In the meantime, the green snakes had coiled themselves around BB.'s forearms. 'They're giving me a cuddle, guys. Would you like to hold one?'

Rose and Sandy shook their heads, and Rose quietly responded. 'The only snakes we like handling come in the little plastic packets at the supermarket.'

Nic returned. 'They're on the way, so we can hang around here or head back to Busselton. What do you guys want to do?'

Rose nodded, then looked at Sandy. 'Busselton, please, we haven't seen the rest of the shops.'

'And you, BB?'

'I'll stay here with these two snake beauties. Besides, I've like got a frog in my pocket. I wouldn't be able to sit down in the car as it might get squished.'

'No worries. Just get an Uber or cadge a lift back. We'll see you later.' Nic, Rose and Sandy returned to the Kombi, and then he drove back to the motel.

A couple of hours later, they were sitting in the restaurant having dinner and BB had not yet appeared. Nic had also noticed Janie wasn't there either. He called the manager over to them. 'Is Janie not working tonight?'

'No, sorry, she said she had something important to do and needed to meet with someone.'

'OK, do you know where, or who with?'

'Nope, sorry.' Nic nodded. 'One last question. Where does Janie's father work? She's told me, but I've forgotten.'

'Oh, we're so proud of our Marc Nelson. He's an associate professor in the Life Sciences Department at Curtin University. He's the go-to guy for reptiles here in Western Australia.'

Rose looked up at the manager. 'Sorry, I have a question. What type of car does Janie drive?'

'I think it's a green '77 Holden Sandman. Her father painted it the same colour as those little green tree frogs she loves and gave it to her on her twenty-first birthday.'

Rose nodded. 'Good to know, and thanks.'

They finished dinner, and it was getting dark. Nic called BB's mobile, but there was no answer. He suspected that BB was with Janie, so he returned to the office manager and had him call her mobile. There was no answer on her phone either. Nic called Chewy.

'Hey mate, sorry about calling late again, but can you triangulate a mobile signal? I'm worried that BB has gone vigilante on me and wants to rescue Lucille.'

'No worries. There are still some black spots out that so it might take a couple of hours to track them down. I'll keep on it. Do you know where he last had his mobile turned on?'

Nic nodded. 'Try the Margaret River Airport first, and then see if you can find a number for Janie Nelson. I suspect they are together.'

'Right. I'll start there.'

In the morning Rose and Sandy met with Nic in his room. 'Chewy has found that the last signal was from a tower off Yoongarillup Road. It's down near the Fish Road Nature Reserve.'

Rose nodded. 'That's not good. Janie said there was a back gate from the nature reserve to the reptile farm. Have you tried his number this morning?'

'Not yet. I'll text in case he's got the ringer off.'

Nic sent: '??'

They anxiously waited, and a text returned: '!'

Nic called his number, and it connected. 'What's going on B.B? Where are you?'

'Janie and I are at the back of the farm. Roxy is here too, as she wanted to help out. She's like Lucille's best friend. We drove in through the nature reserve, and I spent the night in the front seat of her Sandman. We're going to rescue Lucille. It's like not my fault, Nic. They grabbed me at the airport and I couldn't say no.'

'Please wait there. The Parks and Wildlife raiding the property this morning at nine-thirty.'

'What if Jim and Desmond try to escape out this way? Can't we like stop them?'

'No, definitely not. They've got nowhere to go. I'll let you know when we get down there. We'll also be coming in with the Police, and an ambulance, just in case Jim and Desmond do something stupid with the venomous snakes.'

'OK, and don't forget his dogs, Burt and Ernie. They could be trained killers.'

'Just keep safe, and keep out of the way.'

'Ok, and by the way, Janie's got a gun.'

'Damn it, but thanks for telling me. What type?'

'It's a Browning Lightweight Lever Action. She's only ever used it at the Rifle Club and forgot it was in the car. There's a locked box built into the Sandman's roof. She keeps it stored there when it's not at the club.'

'Is she there with you?'

'Yes, she is.'

'Can you put her on, please?'

BB handed the phone over. 'Hello, Mr Thorn. I heard that question, and sorry, I forgot it was in the car.'

'OK, but it changes things, Janie. They might want to go to the next step with the raid if they know you have a gun. I would assume Desmond would be carrying one.'

'Desmond goes to the same Rifle Club as my father and me. They might have about six around the place.'

'Right. Can you to do something for me? Take out all the bullets, bury them near the car, and put the gun back into the safe. If Desmond sees that you are armed, it changes everything.'

'What do I bury it in? We only have our clothes.'

'Has BB still got the trilby with him? Use that. I'll buy him a new one.'

'OK, so it's eight a.m. now. Do we wait another hour and then start going in for Lucille?'

Nic shook his head. 'No, stay where you are, please. I'll get someone from the Parks and Wildlife to come in that way so you can go in with them.'

'OK, we'll see you when this is all over.'

lvis was now heading to the reptile farm and they collected the Parks and Wildlife Team along the way. There was now a convoy of Police cars, an ambulance and two Parks and Wildlife Land Cruisers, led by Elvis, driving a sleek black Porsche Cayenne, He was having trouble keeping the speed under the speed limit.

Nic began to coordinate the raid with the Officer in Charge: 'Yes, it's coming to a head today. Nope, no guns. We're not armed, however, we have Intel that Jim and Desmond have legal possession of at least six rifles on site. There is also a young woman there, Lucille. She's the adopted daughter. When we visited two days ago, there were only two pits with snakes, but they are venomous. There would be anti-venom on site if needed.'

Nic disconnected, and Rose looked at him. 'You just lied to the authorities.'

'Sort of, but I said we are not armed, and that's the truth.'

Sandy piped up. 'Janie's got a gun. Aerosmith '89, I think.'

'Yep, so if I start singing '*run away, run away, run away*' it doesn't mean you should stand there and listen to my warbling. Start running away.'

Sandy nodded. 'What about BB? He said Roxy and Janie were with him What are they going to be doing?'

'Nothing. Hopefully, they will stay where I told them to and hope he keeps it all under control.'

Rose shook her head. 'Remember when you were twenty? Those hormones were raging through your little Nic Thorn teenage body. This guy has just spent the night with two girls, and wants to save someone he's only known for three days.'

Nic sighed. 'I never said what I do was meant to be easy, did I?'

CHAPTER 10

The convoy slowed, and the second Land-cruiser peeled off Acton Park Road into the scrub to meet with BB. A few minutes later, the remaining vehicles turned left into Fish Road, moments away from starting the raid.

The cars pulled to a stop just short of the reptile farm, where the groups climbed out of their vehicles and assembled at the gate. The Officer in Charge made a phone call, and he was given the green light.

The lead officer snapped the lock off the entrance with bolt cutters, and the Parks and Wildlife vehicle drove in. Rose and Sandy were directed to stay in the Porsche, so Elvis did a U-turn and stopped on the verge on the other side of the road.

Nic called BB and he answered. 'Janie's Dad's on his way too. Sorry, I didn't tell you he was coming with the Parks and Wildlife people. You might have some explaining to do......'

The call was abruptly cut off.

Nic rang back, but it didn't answer, and in the meantime, at the front gate, the team made their move:

This is the Department of Parks and Wildlife, and this is a raid. We have a warrant to search the

The group crept toward the Reptile Office, but as there wasn't any movement, the Police jemmied the sliding door open and quickly stepped inside with guns drawn. The place was empty, and all the piles of papers were gone.

Nic stepped in behind them and moved directly towards the cement pits in the other room. He went quickly over to one of the half walls and looked in.

'Body. We've got a body in here. It's Jim.'

The ambulance officers assisted Nic in dropping a ladder into the pit, and they carefully approached the prostrate man. Nic pointed towards the loose straw strewn across the back wall. 'There's Adders and Vipers in here, so be careful.'

The ambulance officers checked the man for vital signs, announced that there was still a pulse, and carefully turned him over.

Jim's eyes fluttered, and Nic looked at the Ambulance Team. 'Any sign of a bite?'

'Nope, the pulse is strong. If he'd been bitten, it would be erratic. Can you move?'

Jim sat up. 'My boy hits me, he goddam hits me. Then he chucks me over the wall. I'd moved the snakes out of this pit early this morning, but he wouldn't ta known that.'

Nic looked at him. 'You know why we are here, don't you Jim? We found the reptiles at the Margaret River airport. They were in a unit being leased by Sheila.'

Jim sighed. 'Dumb woman. This place was being sold. I signed the paper last night, but my boy and her, gone and stuffed it all up.'

Nic nodded. 'What are you talking about, Jim? Where has Desmond gone? What doesn't he know about?'

Jim sighed. 'He knows nothing. I'd got sick of doing this. I've just chucked it in and will spend my last days fishing in Albany. I've got the Big C mate. Doc says about a year left if I'm lucky. Me boy has taken Lucille, and he's making a run for it.'

Nic nodded again. 'Jim, we've recovered the reptiles in Cairns too, so they'll be coming back. As for the sale, when's that happening?'

'Next month. I git ma money, and I'll be gone. Lucille will be OK. She's a good kid, and there's enough money for me to pay her tuition for a bit. She's going to be a Doctor, but it's too late to save me.'

One of the Police Officers approached Nic after helping Jim out of the pit. 'Nic, there's no sign of Des or Lucille. Maybe they took a back road out?'

'Yep, they could have. It goes out to the Nature Reserve. We sent the second Parks and Wildlife crew through that way. I was talking to my team member, BB Kingsman, but we got cut off.'

Nic ran outside, joined the police and the Parks and Wildlife Officers, and they all piled into the

Land Cruiser, then sped towards the second property.

They arrived, quickly jumped out of the car, forced open the door of the building and stepped inside. It too was tidy, clean and empty. Nic tried BB's mobile again, and this time, it answered. 'What happened, BB? We got cut off.'

BB whispered. 'Sorry. It's like a standoff happening here. Desmond is here, along with Lucille. They came on foot. He has his snake with him, Dallas the Dugite. He's not going to give up without a fight.'

'Where are you?'

'In the Sandman with Roxy and Janie.'

'What about Janie's dad and the Parks and Wildlife crew?'

'We haven't like seen them.'

'OK. What's Desmond doing?'

'He's like twirling the snake about like it's a lasso. He's going to get bitten.'

'OK. I'm going to ask you to take the gun out. Can you get to it?'

'Yes, Janie's in the back. We can't like to get to the bullets, though. You told us to bury them.'

'I know BB, and that's still a good thing. Can you see if Desmond has a gun?'

'I would like to say not. He wouldn't be twirling the snake around if he did.'

'Can you put Janie on again, please?'

BB handed over the phone. 'Hi, Mr Thorn. It sounds like you have a plan. Are you far away?'

'I think about five minutes, we're on the dirt track coming towards you.'

'OK. You want me to get the gun and do what? There are no bullets.'

'Desmond wouldn't know that, so please get it out, put it together and step out of the back. BB and Roxy will need to lock you outside. Can you do that?'

'Yes, and I don't know how much longer Lucille can keep like standing next to Desmond without getting bitten.'

'We'll be there soon. How long will it take to get it from the safe?'

'I did it whilst you were talking to me.'

'OK then. Go.'

Janie gave the phone back, then kicked out the double rear doors of the Sandman and stepped out wielding the gun. Desmond saw her instantly and laughed. 'I've seen you shoot, Janie. You can't hit the side of a barn with a Gatling gun.'

Janie grinned. 'I know that Desmond, but I only need one shot, and from here, where do you want it? Between the eyes, or between your legs. You choose.'

'You're bluffing, girl.'

Janie pulled back the gun lever, snapped it into place, and then pointed it at him. 'Let her go, Desmond, and I don't mean the snake. It's the four of us against you.'

Janie took her aim. 'And just so you know Dallas is a female, so I'm sure she'll help us too. Look at the length of the tongue tines. I thought you were a snake expert, everyone knows that about the tines.'

Desmond looked at her, then at Lucille. 'Dallas is a boy's name. Everyone knows that. He's my little man.'

BB realised Janie was stalling for time. 'Hey Desmond, have you seen the latest Jurassic Park movie? Claire Dearing, the Park Manager, the actor's name is Dallas Howard.'

Desmond decided to take a closer look at the snake's tongue, and it recoiled and bit him on the face. 'Crap, I've been bit.'

BB and Roxy realised that Janie had the upper hand, and they moved over to Lucille.

They gathered in an embrace and then looked at Desmond. He dropped to the ground and let go of the snake. 'I don't feel so good.'

Janie smiled. 'Stay still, lie down, and start praying. Where did Dallas go?'

'Next ta me...'

'It's a he, Desmond. You can't tell from just looking at the tongue. I made it up.'

Desmond lay on the ground and mumbled. 'But why call her Dallas? It's a place in America. I wanted to get over there, but now I will die here in this dump.'

Nic and his team finally arrived, and quickly climbed out of the car, He noticed Desmond lying on the ground. 'What happened? Was he shot?'

'No, Dallas the Dugite bit him. Do you have any anti-venom?'

'Yes, we do.'

One of the Parks and Wildlife Officers collected the First Aid kit and the anti-venom. 'When did he get bitten, what bit him and how long ago?'

BB looked down at Desmond. 'On the face, it was a Dugite. It's still around here somewhere so be careful. Oh, there he is, slithering off towards the Sandman, As for the bite, maybe a couple of minutes before you arrived.'

BB carefully bypassed the slowly moving snake, went to the back of the car, collected the inner sleeve of a sleeping bag, and picked up a forked stick. 'Here Dallas, come out and play. I've like got like a lovely soft bag to wrap you up in.'

Janie pointed towards the snake. 'You're not going to catch it, are you?'

'There's like the bitey part and the tail end. I think I know like which is which as I've dealt with bigger teeth than that on the Tasmanian Devils.'

BB moved towards the snake, dropped the forked branch into its docile head, held his foot against the neck, picked it up and carefully dropped it into the bag. It all took less than a minute.

Nic looked at him. 'Nice catch, BB.'

'We have snakes in Tasmania. So, I kept thinking about their Tasmanian cousins, and they're much less nasty than this little critter.'

The young women gathered around and hugged him again, and the First Aid officer looked up. 'I'll get the Ambulance to come down here from the farm. It will collect Jim and take them both to the hospital. The anti-venom has been administered.'

The group then heard another vehicle approaching, and this time, it was from the nature reserve. The car stopped, and three people got out. Janie ran to her father, gave him the gun, and hugged him. 'Thanks, but no thanks, these things are about death, not life.'

Nic walked up to the recently arrived group. 'So, what happened?'

'We got lost.'

CHAPTER 11

A day later Nic visited Jim and Desmond in the hospital. Desmond was fortunate as it was only a glancing bite, and he was ready to be discharged. Jim, however, had a broken rib and a broken arm. They were side by side in the hospital beds.

'Hi, Thorn. This guy over there, he snores. First, he chucks me in me snake pit, and then he snores like a swamp pig.'

Desmond snorted and looked over at his father. 'You sold up?'

'Yep. End of this month I get mi money.'

'What about my share?'

'Nope, Desmond. You'll find yours in the bottom of the snake's pit. You can stay on working there too if you want, I don't care. I'm off da Albany as soon as they let me out of here.'

The younger man glared at him but said nothing more.

Nic smiled. 'I think you don't have to worry about working under new management at the farm for a while, Desmond. You've got a stint coming for you at Hakea Prison. Maybe they'll let you smuggle in Dallas the Dugite for company with all the other snakes living there.'

Desmond stared out the window, then turned back to them. 'Nunya business.'

Nic continued. 'Lucille has received a Medical Scholarship at Launceston General Hospital in Tasmania. Her friend Roxy has one, too. They leave with BB on Friday.'

Nic approached Jim to shake his hand, and Jim raised his hand to his eyes to wipe tears away.

'You know I hoped my kid wasn't behind all the smuggling. Maybe I was stupid, and he baited my two dogs. Ya can pick your friends, but you can't pick your kin, right?'

Nic nodded. 'Best of luck to you, Jim, and I hope you catch a big one before the end comes.'

Nic left the room, leaving Desmond staring out the window and Jim staring at a coil of clear tubing hanging from the wall.

'I miss me snakes already.'

Nic returned to the Ithaca Motel, settled the bill and BB was pleased to be returning to Tasmania as he would be helping Roxy and Lucille settle into their new lifestyle.

BB was excited at the prospect. 'Nic, I haven't been home in weeks and weeks. I can like hear the little Tassie Devils like crying out my name.'

'It's only been just over a week. I thought you'd decided to stay here to go rocking out with the quokkas on Rotto. What's the hurry? It's still so cold down there at the moment.'

Sandy interrupted them. 'How will you ever get those two to go outside, BB? It never gets above twenty degrees in Tasmania.'

BB shook his head. 'Not true. We like had three days in December above thirty a couple of years ago. It caused all the snow caps and ice creams to melt.'

Nic smiled. 'Anyway, did you fly from Hobart and leave your Kombi somewhere safe?'

BB nodded. 'I flew from Lonnie, left it at a mates place. I can't wait to get back, and drive them around to show them all the secrets of home.'

Nic nodded. 'Maybe we'll get back there one day, but meantime I've been given the go-ahead to investigate a guy purporting to sell vintage wine stock at Margaret River. It's a little bit closer than Tasmania, and a bit warmer.'

Rose sighed. 'And?'

Nic looked at Rose and Sandy. 'Well, my connoisseurs of cardboard chardonnays, we're setting up an investigation of an oenophile. He's certainly got people worried around here.'

Sandy looked at Nic. 'What's a one-yo-file? It sounds like something you find in a nail salon.'

Nic continued. 'It's someone that knows a lot about wine, then they add in access to an exclusive range of wines, throw money around, and turn up in Margaret River undercutting the local markets. Some people get very anxious, and we'll be representing those people.'

Rose nodded again. 'And I bet those people make the best whiners too.'

Nic grinned. 'Hey, that's quite good, Rose. I might use that one.'

BB looked at them. 'I could stay here with you guys if you need me to.'

Nic shook his head. 'Nup, but thanks for the offer. Let's get the little devil to the airport before he changes his mind.'

BB paused. 'How about you drop me off at the Busselton station and I'll catch the train to Perth instead.'

Nic nodded. 'Sounds like a plan. Thanks again for all your help with this one, and for being a seriously good snake snatcher.'

The group walked to the train station and said their goodbyes.

BB only had a small backpack, and Sandy wanted to check if he was trying to smuggle a quokka back to Tasmania with him. They waved BB off and started walking back to the motel.

Rose stopped mid-stride. 'As we've already checked out of the Motel, how can we walk back there and check back in? They might be full up, and we've lost our driver.'

Nic grinned. 'Nope, it's all good. I called Elvis and he'll pick us up back at the motel, then we'll go down to the Lookarwi Resort in Margaret River.'

Rose looked at Nic. 'I hope it's a five-star.'

'It could be six stars, but I haven't seen it yet.'

Elvis collected them, but when they stopped at the first red traffic light, he suddenly climbed out without saying a word and walked into a bottle shop.

Nic turned around to face Rose and Sandy. 'Look what you've done, even Elvis can't stand your whining about the standard of the hotel rooms.'

Elvis returned a moment later carrying a bottle of red wine, and Nic read the label out loud.

'This is a 2005 Chateau Mouton Rothchild. It's about sixteen hundred dollars a bottle. The local wines down this way only go for a max five hundred.'

Rose nodded. 'So, what's the scam? They put the bottles in soapy water, slide the labels off, then swap them onto another wine bottle full of blackberry juice?'

'Not quite. It might be more than that.'

Elvis drove the 40 minutes from Busselton to the town of Margaret River, took the left turn onto Boodjidup Road and slowed down as they passed the turn-off to a Raptor Wildlife Centre.

Rose had noticed. 'That's not fair. You told us there would be no more shovelling guano, and we just happened to pass another bird sanctuary.'

Nic nodded. 'Yep, and that's where you and Sandy will end up if I can't convince the guys at Voyager Estate Winery, that we are legitimate wine connoisseurs. We're meeting with one of their vintners to give us a course in wine appreciation tomorrow.'

Sandy grinned. 'Wow, that's early to start drinking, but I guess it's always after five somewhere in the world.'

Elvis shook his head. 'I can drop them at the Raptor Centre now if you like.'

They arrived at the resort ten minutes later, and Elvis parked the car in the waiting bay.

Two porters helped Rose and Sandy from the back seat, and a third collected their luggage.

Rose smiled at the quality of the decor. 'Damn it, Nic, we left our Louis Vuitton luggage behind in Brisbane. It would have suited this place.'

They went into the foyer, and there was a cascading waterfall behind the reception desk. Nic glanced at Rose. 'Don't get any ideas, Rose.'

Elvis looked at him, wondering what the comment meant. 'Don't worry mate. I'll show you the YouTube link later.'

Nic completed the paperwork. 'Three separate rooms this time, guys.'

Sandy grinned. 'Does that mean you have to double bunk with Elvis?'

Nic shook his head. 'Nope, he's staying offsite. We have to appear that we're all here from the same Wine Company, so that's the reason for the separate rooms. I haven't come up with a name for our Business yet. Chewy is still working on the backstory and our portfolios.'

Rose grinned. 'Sandy and I could come up with some good names if you give us an hour or two in the day spa.'

Nic smiled. 'Chewy will get back to me later tonight. We'll meet for an early breakfast and can go through it all then, but meantime, let's go to dinner.'

Rose looked at Sandy. 'But we haven't got anything to wear. Have you seen the décor in this place? We feel a little under-dressed.'

Nic nodded. 'So I noticed. I contacted a couture shop called Sunflowers in Margaret River. They've already delivered a selection of clothes for you and put them into your room. You can wear their range whilst we're looking into this investigation.'

Rose smiled. 'How did you know our dress sizes? Oh, that's right, you buy stuff, sell stuff and know stuff. It'll be a struggle, but we'll be their clothes' models, but just make sure we get paid as models, not just as your associates this time.'

Nic nodded. 'I still haven't paid you guys anything yet.'

Rose continued. 'Nope, we have put everything on your Credit Card instead, including the hour session in the day spa in less than forty-five minutes. So, we'll have to eat in the clothes we have on now if that's OK.'

'Sure guys, enjoy it at my expense.'

Rose smiled. 'We always do.'

When they met Nic for breakfast, Rose and Sandy were dressed in classic dark blue suits from the Sunflowers range which caused stares from some of the gentlemen diners.

One was overheard saying to his wife, '*You never wear an outfit like that for me for breakfast.*' The woman replied, '*Well, you never look like him in the morning either, dear.*'

CHAPTER 12

Nic was still smiling at the comment as Rose and Sandy sat down to join him.

Rose nodded. 'So, what's this one about? Has Chewy been in touch?'

'Yep. There's a big wine auction tomorrow at the Margaret River Hotel. About fifty bidders are expected, and big money is on offer. It's just one guy's collection of mainly French wines. His name is Lord Julian Somersby-Kent, and he's the Duke of some land holdings in England. He lives in a Castle of a hundred rooms or so. Rumour has it that there is something not quite kosher with the collection, but no one is game to say anything. Other than that, no one has ever seen the guy.'

Rose leaned forward. 'So that's the scam? Pretending to be someone else? Why can't they open the wine to find out?'

Nic continued: 'The bottles are mainly collectors' items and held for storage, never to be opened. Some of the wines are over fifty years old. It's about the prestige of owning rather than the drinking.'

Sandy nodded. 'I think I get it, but surely the collection is only as legitimate as the seller's integrity, just like buying art. A fake is a fake, and as Rose's folks know since they ended up with that dodgy painting, but how do you dodgy up the wine?'

Nic leaned forward. 'There are a couple of ways. A couple of years ago, Cambodia had a South Australian Penfolds Wine scam. That was a labelling issue as the scammers replaced the labels on their wine bottles and sold them in a local market as *'buy your Penfolds bargain here'*. They were caught, but not before some money had changed hands.'

Rose nodded. 'True. They even came up with a name for it, 'Benfolds'. It sounds like an American music trio, but they're called Ben Folds Five. That was an odd name as there are only three of them.'

Nic was about to congratulate her knowledge of the random music fact when a well-dressed man approached their table: 'Good morning, Sir, Ladies. My name is Viscount Siimon Somersby-Kent, and I believe you are here for the wine auctions. We appreciate your attendance.'

Nic stood up and shook his hand. 'Nice to make your acquaintance, Lord Somersby-Kent. I am Lord Nicolas, Earl of Crawley, Lord of Highclere Castle, and these two ladies are part of the house management of my castle. I have brought along them with me.'

'Well, again thank you for your patronage, my Lord. I look forward to vigorous bidding from you.' The young man moved away and onto another table.

Nic waited for him to move out of earshot. 'I bet he's part of the scam and not a real Viscount. He should have known I would not have breakfast with my house staff if I were an Earl.'

Rose shook her head. 'That's a bit of a stretch. Maybe he was too polite to say anything, or maybe he had something else on his mind, like running a phony wine auction.'

Nic continued. 'Besides that, he can't be a Downton Abbey fan, either. Highclere Castle is where the filming was done.'

Sandy whispered. 'You dope. You said that we weren't going to use that.'

Nic nodded. 'Not quite. I said we might use it for the reptile thing, but we didn't need to.'

Sandy continued. 'I wouldn't have picked you for a Downtonian anyway. I love some of Lady Grantham's quotes: *I know several couples who are perfectly happy; they haven't spoken in years'* or '*Nothing succeeds like success.'*

Rose looked at them, 'You two are at it again. I read the brief but didn't get into that TV show. I thought Sandy was watching the re-runs of Upstairs Downstairs.'

The man then took control of the breakfast crowd: 'Ladies and Gentlemen, for those who do not know who I am, I am Viscount Siimon Somersby-Kent, Lord of Menloch Castle. I am here in your glorious country for the prestige wine auctions at the Margaret River Hotel. Viewing commences at eleven on Friday morning, with the main auction commencing at noon on Saturday.'

He turned and exited.

Nic nodded towards Sandy. 'Can you follow him discretely? See what he drives or where he goes.'

Sandy got up, exited through the foyer and returned a few minutes later. 'I lost him, but he wasn't driving. Maybe on foot?'

They then heard the recognisable sound of a helicopter taking flight. Nic watched as it moved away. 'OK, guys, it looks like this is the big league.'

Rose nodded. 'So, do you have to become a helicopter pilot for a day?'

'Nope, that's one thing Nic Thorn cannot do. He only flies planes with parachutes in their tails.'

'Don't do that.'

'What's that? Limit myself to planes with parachutes in their tails?'

'Nope, you dope, talk about yourself in the third person.'

Elvis then collected them and they headed to the Voyager Estate.

Rose smiled. 'So, are we off to learn about wines now?'

Nic nodded. 'Yep, but remember there'll be no drinking for you.'

Sandy was shaking her head. 'This isn't fair, as we're so disappointed we're not allowed to savour the wines. How are you going to make it up to us?'

Elvis looked over. 'Mr Nic, I only need to keep driving and can drop them off at the Raptor Bird Sanctuary. I'll have them back shovelling guano in no time.'

'Thanks, but we're good. I need them to tend to my every need, like preparing my clothes for the day, keeping everything washed and smelling nice, roasting my marshmallows, and as a special treat, I'm allowing them to attend the wine auction.'

Rose called out from the back seat. 'That's not what house managers do, we are the seneschals and we supervise the domestics, in case they have a domestic. Do we have the special names yet?'

'Yep, you're called Miss-*Fire*, and Sandy is Miss-*Led*.'

'Ha, funny. So what are they?'

'Nope, just use Miss Jones and Miss Smith. Alternate between them if you like and first names will not be needed. If anybody presses the issue, refer them to the Lord Almighty.'

'God?'

'No, to me. I am, after all, Lord Nicolas, Earl of Crawley.'

Sandy grinned. 'OK, we've got it, Lord Voldemort.'

Elvis drove into the Voyager Estate, they stepped from the car, and he went around the back of the complex to find a carpark.

Rose watched him leave. 'Is Elvis joining us? You're going to get mighty lonely drinking all by yourself.'

'Don't worry about me. Besides, I'm not here to drink the wine, only look at it, smell it, sip it, swill it and spit it out.'

'Be serious, Nic. Drinking alcohol can cause people to lose their inhibitions, and we'd hate to see you inhibited, uninhibited, or un-inhabited.' Nic shrugged. 'I'm not as think as you drunk I am.'

They made their way inside the wine-tasting area where a crowd of twenty other patrons was milling around, waiting for the presentation.

Nic nodded towards the young man they met at the Lookarwi Resort and Rose and Sandy tried to ignore him, then noticed he wasn't alone.

Sandy whispered. 'Crikey Nic, I thought when you introduced us to your French friend Benoit Trudeau in Melbourne they broke the good-looking man-mould with him, but that guy standing next to Viscount Siimon Somersby-Kent has just fallen out of the latest Vogue magazine.'

Rose agreed. 'I think we'll have you get to know them better for research purposes. Do you think you could ask one of them to take us for a ride in the helicopter?'

Nic whispered back. 'Hey, that's not fair; I thought I was Hemsworthy. On the scale of me to Chris Hemsworth, what number is that guy?'

Rose looked at him, then back at Nic. 'Out of ten? He's an eleven, but Chris H is a fourteen anyway.'

The Viscount came over to them and firmly shook Nic's hand. 'Thank you for coming today, Lord Crawley, and you have brought along your staff too.'

Nic nodded. 'Yes, I've allowed them to attend the auction spectacle. They will not be in the way.'

The man acknowledged his permission and then introduced Nic to his companion. 'Lord Nicolas Crawley, please let me introduce you to Prince Michael of Lyon. He is French and alas, does not speak much English.'

The second man shook Nic's hand and ignored Rose and Sandy. The men then chatted about the Wine Industry, and after a couple of minutes, the little group disbanded.

Rose whispered to Nic. 'My parents forced me to marry Michael, so why couldn't he have been a Prince at least.'

Nic whispered. 'He's not a real prince, they said he was from Lyon in France. The French haven't had a monarchy for over two hundred years.'

Rose shook her head. 'But he's a still prince and one day I hope I'll find my prince, but I'd gratefully accept a marquess or a baron.'

Nic whispered. 'It's a scam, and my Spidey senses tell me it's a very good one.'

Another well-dressed man called the crowd together: 'Good morning Ladies and Gentlemen. My name is Jacob, and I am your sommelier for this presentation. We will be sampling some of the wines most generously provided by Lord Julian Somersby-Kent. Unfortunately, he cannot be with us this morning, however, he has committed to joining us at the pre-auction on Friday. The main auction is on Saturday.'

Nic leaned towards Rose. 'I bet the Lord Somersby-Kent doesn't turn up on Friday or Saturday either.'

The crowd were ushered into the Tasting Area, and the host began again: 'There are two main things to know about tasting wine, and it's not whether one is red and the other white. Number One is Slow Down, and Number Two is Pay Attention.'

The patrons took their seats and were politely updated about the wine districts of France, types of wines and other items of particular interest. Each guest was presented with a notepad and asked to rate the wines. Nic ensured Rose and Sandy were well away from his notes.

The host continued: 'Enjoy the experience, Ladies and Gentlemen, and get your nose into the glass and sniff. Please write down the aroma on your notepad, and we'll all compare notes later. Suck, swish and swallow. We will not be spitting the wine out. I want you to taste it, not waste it.

Take the bread pieces as required, and if you feel it's becoming too much, please stop. We are here to sample the wines and enjoy the process.'

After about 45 minutes of wine tasting, the room was getting rather noisy and robust discussions were commonplace among the attendees. The host then quieted everyone down: 'Ladies and gentlemen, we have a special opportunity here today. A bottle of 2005 Chateau Mouton Rothchild has been provided to sample by Lord Nicolas, Earl of Crawley. This bottle retails for around sixteen hundred dollars. He has offered it here today as a reminder of what you can expect from the wine auction on Friday.'

Rose leaned towards Nic. 'Damn you, Nic. I thought that was ours to drink.'

'It still is. I decanted it into a carafe earlier this morning, poured in a cleanskin, and re-sealed the bottle. It's been breathing for the last fifteen minutes.'

The sommelier announced. 'Please make your way up to the Tasting Desk. This tasting is optional as it is a high-quality product and may not suit your taste. Please do not waste the opportunity, but if you have had enough already, it may not be the ideal time this morning to enjoy this wine.'

Only about five men and two women ventured to the Desk.

Nic hadn't moved, nor Lord Siimon or Prince Michael. Nic whispered to Rose. 'This will be interesting as we should get some reactions straight away. Any decent wine connoisseur will know from the nose that the wine is not French.'

The wine was poured, and most of them followed the process they had just learned. Three of them, however, put the glasses down immediately, and two managed to taste, but didn't complete the swallow. A woman drank it down, took one of the other glasses, and drank that too.

The last man spat it back quickly into the glass.

The host saw the commotion, prepared his sample, raised the glass to the light, swilled it around, and put it back on the table.

'Lord Crawley, you are either trying to dupe us here or have been duped yourself. This is not French wine, nor is it fifteen years old.'

CHAPTER 13

Nic stood up quickly. 'I'm so sorry. It appears that a prank was played on me, however your people decanted the wine. Did they tamper with it?'

The host glared at him, then turned to his audience: 'Well, Ladies and Gentlemen, it has been a lesson for us all here this morning. Please don't believe that because you see the open bottle poured; it is what you have paid for. I hope you have enjoyed my presentation, and I look forward to catching up with you all at the first wine auction on Friday.' The man shook a few guests' hands and then exited the room.

Rose whispered to Nic. 'What was the point of that charade?'

Nic nodded to Sandy to follow them again while Rose and Nic entered the foyer for privacy. 'Well, it was just another test.'

Sandy quickly returned, and Nic whispered. 'Did you see what happened to Prince Michael of Lying and Viscount Smooth-Dude?'

'I missed them again. I only got as far as the helicopter pad out the back, but at least we know neither of them is the pilot, so that's good.'

Rose smiled, and Nic noticed. 'Why is that good?' Sandy responded. 'It means that you won't try and take the pilot's place and get us up in one of those over-ambitious eggbeaters. I did manage to find out where they were staying. It's in the Fremantle Harbour.'

'Good work, Sandy. Which one of the handsome dudes told you that?'

'Neither. Elvis was talking to the helicopter pilot.'

Nic nodded. 'Lucky, I stopped Elvis before he left the building. What Hotel are they staying at in Fremantle?'

Sandy grinned. 'They're not in a Hotel, they're *in* the harbour, on a boat, with a helicopter pad on the back.'

'Wow, this *is* the super league, guys. Depending on the size of the craft, you rent those yachts from around fifteen to a hundred thousand per week, plus the crew.'

Rose whispered, 'If this is a scam, Lord Julian is turning over a lot of money to keep up with his expenses.'

'Yep, and I'm still waiting on Chewy to give me the total picture, but at the last auction these guys did in Tokyo, Japan it grossed over five hundred thousand in wine sales. The auction is on the internet. It goes for half an hour and there are English subtitles.'

Sandy nodded. 'Konnichiwa. So, what are we up to for the rest of the day?'

'Well, I'm going back to the resort. Would you like Elvis to drive you around to visit some other wineries? You're both off duty now, so live it up.' Sandy looked at him. 'We've left your Credit Cards in the room safe at the resort, so unless you can spot us some cash, we're coming back with you.'

'That's good then. Besides, I want to take a nap, which means one of you will have to turn my bed down, and the other iron my pj's.'

'You wish Mr Nic.' It was a man's voice. Nic looked around and saw Elvis.

Elvis nodded at Rose and Sandy, then to Nic. 'I found out some more gossip, too. Let's return to the Porsche, and I'll run you guys back.'

They went out to the carpark and found Jacob leaning against the car. 'So, Lord Nicolas, Earl of Crawley, what was the point of the little wine swap in there?'

Nic smiled. 'I thought it put an interesting spin on everything we learned this morning, especially about trusting wine merchants.'

'OK, but since when does Lord Crawley own the castle of Downton Abbey.'

'Right, Jacob. I'm not the owner of the castle, but it is part of a portfolio of the properties owned by the Earl of Carnarvon.'

Jacob shook his head. 'You're supposed to be the Earl of Crawley. Crawley is the family name from the TV series Lord Nicolas.'

Elvis piped up.' Well, my name's not Elvis, nor is this Miss Smith or Jones. We're here to be anonymous bidders at the wine auction. If the sellers knew whom we were representing, it might affect the auction prices.'

The man carefully looked them both over. 'Good point. I'll take my leave now, but there are many prestige wines on offer over the next couple of days. If I find out you're not legitimate buyers, Lord Crawley, you will not be welcome.'

They watched Jacob walk away, moved into their car and headed off towards the resort. After leaving the township, Nic finally spoke: 'Thanks, Elvis, that was close. It's been a while since someone had so quickly picked up on one of my charades. It means I'm getting lazy, and Nic Thorn doesn't like getting lazy.'

Rose called out from the back seat. 'You're doing it again, Nic. Talking about yourself in the third person.'

'Yep, I'm getting lazy everywhere. What have you two turned me into? Quickly, Sandy, throw me one of my idioms or quote from a movie.'

'OK. "We're going to need a bigger boat."'

Nic grinned. 'Ah, that's from Jaws, the greatest fish of all. Thanks, Sandy, I'm back already.'

Rose made a guttural sound. 'Hang on if Elvis isn't your real name, what are we supposed to call you?'

'Elvis is fine, or Colonel Mustard or Colonel Sanders, I don't mind.' He saluted at them in the rear vision mirror.

Rose added. 'Are you even one of Nic's mates? Can you fly a helicopter? Are you even a Colonel? But I think we'll stick with Elvis if that's OK.'

'Thank you, ma'am. Ah-ha-hum. Elvis is in da house, well, in the car anyway.'

Nic interrupted them. 'What else did you find out?'

'Oops, sorry. Well, firstly, their team is just the three men. The pilot is a man for hire, he's a good flyer, an ex-rescue chopper pilot from NSW. He can easily land the four-seater Robinson on the back of the yacht. It's drop off and collect only. He's never been aboard and hasn't seen the elusive Lord Julian Somersby-Kent either, but he knows someone is staying on board.'

'OK, anything else.'

Elvis continued: 'Yes. He's due to collect the wine for the auction from a warehouse at Fremantle and deliver it to the Margaret River Hotel on Friday. He always has one of the other men with him.'

Nic nodded. 'How long did you speak with him?'

'About twenty minutes, but I'd met him years ago. We flew the Erickson helicopters during the New South Wales bushfires in 2001. I piloted 'Elvis' the water bombing helicopter, and that's how I got my name.'

'So, Nic.'

'Yes, Rose?'

'Are we going to have to fly in another helicopter? What are you going to do, steal it and tell everyone you're looking for Skippy the Bush Kangaroo?'

'Nup, it's a long way to fly from here to Waratah National Park in NSW, but thanks for the suggestion. There's no moon tonight, so Elvis and I will take a midnight swim to get a closer look at their yacht moored in Fremantle Harbour.'

Rose sighed. 'C'mon Nic, surely they're about five hundred metres out, and it would be a cold and lonely swim that time of night. Besides, they might see you coming in a boat.'

'We'll get a couple of DPVs and stay under the water.'

Elvis looked over at him. 'It's been a while since I took a Diver Propulsion Vehicle, but I have a mate at the Dive and Ski Shop in Fremantle that can lend them to us for a couple of hours.'

Sandy called out. 'What about the sharks?'

'Good question, Sandy. I can handle Card Sharks and Loan Sharks, and I'm sure the snappy ones are much the same if I make the right deal. After all, I am Nic Thorn.' Nic put his arms forward in the classic flying Superman pose.

They drove to the resort, stepped from the car, and Elvis began to talk with Nic about the swim. 'It's about a three-hour drive to Fremantle from here. I'll pick you up at eight-thirty tonight, which will get us there around midnight.'

'OK, but it's eleven now, so set it up with your diving mate. Take Rose and Sandy with you and spend the afternoon there. Keep it on the down low as it might be a little suspicious if we turn up and pop the DPVs in the water in the middle of the night.'

Elvis nodded. 'I'll go and grab my stuff for tonight and be back in half an hour.'

'No worries. These two will take that long to decide what to wear anyway.'

Sandy scoffed. 'That's not fair. Now we're back here, we can get to the room safe and to your Business Credit Cards.'

Nic nodded. 'Can you at least put together an overnight case, in case we have to overnight?'

Rose nodded. 'Roger that, Nic, or Nic that Roger.'

They watched Elvis drive off, went into the foyer, and Rose suddenly stopped at looked at him. 'If we're going to Fremantle now, how will you get there later?'

'On a bike, Rose.'

'It's over two hundred and seventy kilometres. That's a long ride, even with your skinny legs.'

Nic smiled. 'I'll be riding a Harley Davidson. That big beast out the front is for hire. Harley and Rose, now that's another great song. It's by the band,

'The Black Sorrows'. That's from your era, Rose. It was released in 1990.'

Rose shook her head. 'I wasn't even born.'

'Oh, OK...the next time we're on a driving holiday, I'll upload it to my Spotify, and you can listen to my choice of music.'

Sandy piped up. 'You're on, but everything we've done so far with you has been one big driving holiday.'

'Yep, there is that.'

An hour later, they were having lunch waiting for Elvis. He walked in and sat down with them. 'It's all set up Nic. I've got two wet suits too, miked face masks and fins. All in black.'

'Thanks. Do you know what part of the harbour the yacht is in?'

'Yes, it's about five hundred metres southwest of South Mole Lighthouse. We can park in the carpark, drop off the stuff, or we can go from the Perth Yacht Club Marina. It'll be longer underwater from there.'

'OK, I'll leave it up to you.'

Sandy leaned over to Nic. 'So, what will you need us to do whilst you two are off playing aquamen with flippers and snorkels?'

'You'll be hanging around waiting for us, but thanks, I we don't look anything like Jason Mamoa. I will take that as a compliment.'

Sandy shook her head. 'I was going to say Marine Boy and Flipper.'

CHAPTER 14

They were in the Fremantle harbour, and it was getting near 11 p.m. Nic hadn't yet arrived, although he had responded to an earlier text to meet them by the South Mole Lighthouse. The throbbing noise of a Harley split the silence. Nic rode up, stepped off the motorbike and removed his helmet.

Sandy grinned. 'You made it then, Aqua-boy?'

'Yep, but sorry about the late arrival. Something came with the budgie smuggling stuff. Chewy and I lost track of time. A superhero can't be a superhero all the time. It takes a super-effort and makes me super-tired. I had a nana-nap, and the alarm didn't go off.'

'Well, at least you've got your pop-culture references back.'

'Thanks, Rose. Can you please turn your head as I need to get into my seal suit?'

Rose sighed. 'It's called a wet suit, and we've seen you in one before on that day you went skiff sailing on the Brisbane River. You came back to our house half-dressed, with eyes like pools of dark chocolate.'

Nic grinned. 'So, you only noticed my eyes, but that was different, it was during the day and about thirty degrees. Here it's about fifteen, and I hate getting cold.'

Rose added. 'Stop being a sook. Besides, there's a secret to getting warm once you're in the wet suit. Divers know that.'

'OK, what is it then?' Nic smiled and handed over a headset to Rose.

Rose did a sound check with the microphone. 'Well, once you get in the water, open it at the zip and let some water in. Your body temperature will warm it up soon enough.'

Nic grinned. 'That's not the one I heard, but thanks anyway.'

Rose and Sandy helped to carry the DPVs into the water, and the boys flipped and flopped alongside until they reached some depth. They dove in, prepared themselves, checked their regulators, and gave the women the thumbs up.

Rose called them as they bobbed up and down in the black water. 'I thought you don't do things illegal. Surely boarding a boat in the middle of the night could be considered an act of piracy?'

'Rrrrr...you'rrr right me wee lassy, but we arrrent pirrrates. I've got two legs and don't have a parrot on my shoulder. What about you, Captain Sparrow? Rrrrr.'

Elvis added. 'Nope, I'm not a pirrrrate either, but my favourite alphabet letter is RRRR. Maybe I could be?'

'Stop it you two. I'm serious, and the sound might carry across the water.'

Nic lowered his tone. 'Well, as long as we don't get caught, it should be OK. So, let's get going Captain Ahab, grab the Pequod and beware of any pointy things in the water, especially ones with big teeth.'

This time, Sandy spoke up. 'Rose, we're not going to get any sense from these two seals, but I'll try anyway. I have a couple of questions, Nic. One; do you want us to wait? And Two, what happens if you do get caught?'

'OK, Sandy: One, we won't get caught, and two, come back for us at twelve-thirty. If we're not here, we'll still be out there, swimming with da fishes. Radio silence now, please.'

The men placed their masks on, spoke into the mouthpieces, nodded to each other that they were transmitting, and disappeared under waves. There was barely a ripple as they submerged.

Rose could hear the men breathing and put her hand over the microphone so her comment would not transmit. 'If the water's dark, the night is dark, the boat is dark, and they're in dark wet suits, how do they know where they're going?'

'Good point. We'll have to ask them when they get back.'

'If they get back.'

'Don't say that. Besides, what will we do for fun if Nic goes missing?'

'We'll manage, but we might have to find Nic's elusive twin sister to tell her what happened. We got close to her in Adelaide, and I almost found her on a farm in Murrayville.'

'And you've met Nic's Uncle but weren't formally introduced. You keep calling him "Mr Grumpy Pants."'

Rose sighed. 'And Nic didn't tell me which side of his family he was related to. Let's return to the car and wait, or do you want to do something else?' Sandy nodded. 'Nope, we'd better wait. I wonder if they're there yet.'

Meantime, Nic and Elvis were still underwater and making good time towards the yacht. Nic softly nudged the foot directly in front of his hand, then reached out and slid his finger along his leg as this was their agreed sign of rising. He throttled off his DPV and broke the surface. Elvis rose with him, and they realised they were almost there. Nic moved closer to him and began treading water.

'It's taking longer than I thought, mate, but all looks quiet. We'll board by the rear platform at the waterline. Remember, if it's all going south, bail, and we'll try something else. All we are trying to do here is locate the elusive Lord Julian Somersby-Kent or get his picture.'

'FAB.'

They submerged and rose again at the rear waterline deck, clipping the DPVs to the underside of the plateau with carabiners and slowly eased out of the water. Nic and Elvis sat quietly in their wet suits and removed their flippers, taking it very slowly, knowing any minor movement could be noticed in the soft swell. Nic leaned forward to Elvis. 'Leave if you want or take the next step. Your call.'

Elvis whispered back. 'F.A.B.'

The men raised themselves into crouched positions and slowly made their way onto the main rear deck. The green and red sidelights along the yacht reflected an eerie glow in the water, and fortunately, it was enough to guide them further into the boat.

When they reached amidships, Nic noticed some pamphlets on the galley table, took out his phone from a waterproof pack, shone the torch onto the papers, then held up his finger and stood still.

Elvis stopped and Nic whispered. 'These look old, and might not be used anymore. This would have to be a picture of the real Lord Somersby. Hopefully, it'll be enough to run a facial recognition scan. Let's get out of here.'

Nic slid the papers into the waterproof pack and they backtracked, reached the waterline deck, unclipped the DPVs, donned their flippers, and headed back to shore.

About thirty minutes later, they reached the beach and re-surfaced. Rose and Sandy had waited for them. Rose waded into the water and took their masks. 'How did you go? Remind us again why you couldn't board the yacht in the daytime?'

Nic began to peel off his wetsuit. 'This was more fun. Besides, we didn't need to go that far into the bulkhead or the cabins. I picked up a couple of pamphlets with a picture of who we assume is the real Lord Julian Somersby-Kent. I'll get Chewy to run facial recognition.'

Sandy nodded. 'Can we go to the Hotel now?'

'Yep, did you find us somewhere to stay? I forgot to check. I must be getting c....old.'

Rose nodded. 'We're staying at Rydges, but you two are much closer for a night in the old Fremantle Gaol after pulling a caper like that.'

Elvis looked at Rose, 'RRR, that's not fair RRRose. We didn't break and enter as the yacht wasn't locked.'

Rose shook her head. 'Well, you stole the papers.'

'True, but it looks like they were only trash anyway. We did them a favour.'

Sandy shook her head at them. 'I'm too tired to argue. It's already tomorrow, and I wouldn't say I like it being tomorrow without having gone to bed whilst it was still today.'

Elvis nodded. 'FAB.'

They packed the car and motored off.

In the morning, Rose and Sandy were in the restaurant having breakfast, but Nic had not yet arrived.

Elvis ambled in. 'I'm getting too old for this crap.'

Rose smiled. 'How long have you been working with Nic?'

'About ten years, but he rarely comes over this way anymore. I've also worked with Chewy and Nic's sister, but that was years ago.'

Rose stopped eating. 'So, you've met Nic's sister. What does she look like? Nic won't let us meet her. He reckons she'll spill all the Nic Thorn secrets.'

'I never actually met her. She spent most of the time disguised as an old man, and it was a good disguise. She nodded and snorted a lot, too, but never spoke.'

'OK, do you have any background gossip on Nic we don't know? Like why he was dishonourably discharged from ASIO?'

Elvis looked at Rose. 'Whoa...who told you that?'

'Dave, our neighbour from next door. He once took a phone call from our Uncle Albert and told him he'd done a Probity Check on Nic.'

Elvis leaned in closer. 'Well, I can tell you that's not entirely true. I will tell you this...' but he stopped mid-sentence as Nic had approached them.

'Morning guys. I slept like a big, soggy log. I dreamt of singing a duo with Feargal Sharkey in a dark, soggy place. I think it was 'Mack the Knife'... Oh, the shark babe, has such teeth dear....'

'It's too early for that.'

Nic shrugged. 'Sorry, Elvis.'

Sandy stretched and swept her shoulder-length blonde hair into a ponytail. 'I have a very serious question to ask you, Elvis.'

'Oh?'

'What was with the F.A.B. last night? I thought that was just something those Thunderbirds puppets said to each other. I didn't think it was a real thing.'

'Actually, it is, but it's not. It's supposed to mean 'Fully Acknowledged Brief' or something like that. It's an alternative to saying 'Roger that' all the time. I lost a hundred-dollar bet with a mate of mine when he showed me that the guy from the Thunderbirds TV Show had made it up.'

Nic overheard. 'So, F.A.B. ain't so FAB. I always thought it was the stuff you use when ironing your clothes.'

Rose shook her head. 'That's Fabulon, you dope.'

Nic shrugged. 'Anyhow, we've got to get back to Margaret River. Who wants to ride the Harley back?' Nic looked over at Rose. 'Sorry, Rose, there are too many turns in the road. I know you've ridden one before, but that was in a straight line.'

'Damn you, Nic.'

'Only kidding. The Harley owner lives here in Fremantle, and I did him a favour by bringing it back for him.'

They checked out of the Hotel, made the two-hour drive to the resort at Margaret River, and Elvis dropped them off. 'I'll pick you up tomorrow around ten for the first auction. Call me if you need me. Elvis has left the building.'

They watched him drive away, and Nic sat down. 'So what do you guys want to do with the rest of the day? We haven't got the car, but there's a Courtesy Bus that can pick us up. We can do a half-day winery tour or visit the Mammoth Caves. When in Rome....go spelunking.'

Rose looked at Sandy, then back to Nic. 'They do half-day spa and wellness treatments here. It includes a milk bath and a Geisha massage, and after spending a cold night in Fremantle harbour, you could at least spot us for that.'

'OK, so how about we do a little hike, then do the spa thing?'

'So, you'll do it?'

'The hike yep, the massage thing in the bath milk, nope. I don't like being touched, and I'm lactose intolerant.'

Rose punched him in the arm. 'No, you're not.'

'Yow, what was that for?'

'Oh, just checking about you not liking being touched.'

Nic rubbed his bicep. 'Let's meet in the restaurant at about six, and I'll take you through tomorrow's play. Chewy might have a report back to me about the reclusive Lord by then.'

At 6 p.m., they met back in the restaurant for dinner. 'It's your last chance to savour the Margaret River wines, so select wisely. I used to think drinking wine was bad for me, so I gave up thinking.'

Rose sighed. 'Tell us, did Chewy find anything from the picture of the Lord on the pamphlet?'

'Yep. It turns out it was a picture of the actual Lord Julian Somersby-Kent, and he does have a son, Viscount Siimon Somersby-Kent, so that makes it very interesting. Neither of them has any type of online profile, so the only way to confirm it is to visit his castle and ring the doorbell.'

Sandy rubbed her hands together. 'Woo Hoo, so we're finally going overseas. The U.K. might be a bit cold this time of year, but a long trip in First Class for us might keep us happy for a while.'

Nic shrugged. 'I hate to disappoint you, but Chewy called the local Police in Galway, Ireland and was told Menloch castle was a ruin. There's no record of a Menloch Castle anywhere else in the UK either.'

Nic put his hand up, the waiter came over, took their orders and poured them each a glass of the house red wine. Rose swilled it in the glass, took a sip, and nodded. 'Hey, this is a nice drop. So, it's a scam and a really good one, then?'

'We don't know that yet either. There is a real Lord Julian and his son, Lord Siimon. There is a

Prince Michael, but not of Lyon, France. Lyon is the surname.'

Rose smiled. 'OK then. We have to stay here for another couple of days, then go to the UK to find the reclusive Lord Somersby–Kents, and another case is closed, then we return home to Brisbane.'

'Nope to that. We're heading off to the next investigation. We've been asked to have a close look into the budgie smugglers, so we're off to Adelaide, then we fly up to Broken Hill where the budgies are apparently being captured.'

Rose added. 'Did you just say a closer look into budgie smugglers?

Nic smiled. 'Wow, no reaction from you guys about returning to Adelaide?'

Sandy nodded. 'Nope, you said before that you'd been talking to Driver, so Rose checked out where the best place for budgie breeding was. We already knew.'

'So, you're both up to it?'

Rose nodded, then added. 'As long as you aren't flying us there in one of your little flying machines.'

'Deal, but you might have to share the plane with a doctor. It will be the Royal Flying Doctor Service at your service. Will you be able to handle that?'

Sandy nodded. 'Deal. Anyhow, what's on for the auction tomorrow then?'

'I don't know yet. Chewy couldn't find anything else about the event apart from what's been posted online, so we'll keep saying that I'm the Lord, and you're my servals ...servants... seneschals.'

Sandy shook her head. 'No, we're not as we've just resigned as you don't give us enough to do. Anyway, I've got another question.'

Nic nodded. 'Oh, oh. Hit me with it, Sandy.'

'It's not that bad. Back at the auction, you said you'd decanted the bottle of red wine. Do we get to taste it?'

'What do you think of the one that you're drinking? It's got a nice nose, swills nicely around the glass, has good colour, and has a silky flavour on the back of the palate. Enjoy, as it's worth about two hundred dollars a sip.'

CHAPTER 15

Elvis was waiting for them in the foyer at 10 a.m. as arranged. Nic was dressed in an Armani black suit, and Rose and Sandy wore matching outfits.

Elvis shook his head. 'C'mon guys, I've put on my one and only suit, and you three are dressed like that at ten o'clock in the morning.'

'The clothes maketh the man, Elvis. It's all about the show, and we'll need to make it a good one today and tomorrow, and I didn't bring a suit for you.'

'That's OK, Mr Nic. I'm at least wearing a cravat.'

Sandy grinned. 'Brad Pitt wears those things, and Cary Grant did too.'

'Thanks, Sandy. So, Mr Nic, are we going to the Margaret River Hotel?'

'Yep. We've got to get there early to make a good impression. I'll need you to hang around just in case Jacob asks too many questions. Remind him that I'm a legitimate buyer, and you represent some of the world's biggest buyers. Don't repeat the name as it might appear too obnoxious.'

They drove off and entered the wine action preview area an hour later. Lord Siimon and Prince Michael welcomed everyone, took their details, and as they entered, requested all mobile phones be turned off, not turned to silent.

Rose hesitated as she turned off her phone, and Nic noticed. 'Chewy has set up an online wine connoisseur profile under the name of Lord Nicolas Crawley and it mentions he's in Perth on holiday with his house management staff.'

'Yes, but it's still nerve-racking pretending you're someone else.'

Nic grinned. 'What about you, Sandy?'

'I'm good, but I can't take my eyes off Prince Michael. I've seen him somewhere before, but I can't remember where. If I take a picture, could Chewy run the facial thingy over it?'

'Yep, take Rose with you and butter him up. If that doesn't work, remind him how you might have contracts with the Victoria's Secret models and maybe they want to use males now, too.'

'I don't think that will work. Any other ideas?'

'Nup. You could just ask him.'

Rose and Sandy went off toward Prince Michael and came back almost immediately. Rose whispered. 'We got it Nic.'

'What did you do then? Use Victoria's Secret or the good-looking man?'

Rose grinned. 'Neither. We just asked Jacob to take a selfie and swapped the camera around. He was too busy posing at the camera and didn't notice.'

'Great, I'll send it off to Chewy.' Nic took her phone, opened it with the password, and sent the email.

Sandy looked at him. 'How did you do that? I've even changed the password from last time, you guessed it.'

'Well, Sandy, you might need to change it again as I watched you keying it.'

'Damn you, Nic.'

'Hey Sandy, that's my line... Damn you, Nic.'

The auction was getting closer, and Rose noticed the change in the room's atmosphere. 'Are you planning on buying something?'

Nic whispered. 'Probably, but it depends on how I go. I might get you to do some bidding.'

Rose continued. 'But what if you and I compete against each other? And what about Sandy?

Nic nodded. 'It won't matter as it'll just drive the price higher, but I have something else in mind for Sandy to do.'

Nic looked around at the audience. 'There's quite a good turnout so far. I guess about sixty people, and this is just the preview as the main auction event is tomorrow.'

They took their seats, and Nic was in the middle. Sandy whispered. 'You didn't have to register as a bidder or get a paddle?'

'Not with this one, but I will tomorrow. That is the one for general admission, whereas this one was by invitation only.'

Jacob, the presenter from the wine tasting, moved up to the lectern: 'Ladies and gentlemen, thank you for your attendance today. My name is Jacob Kreik. I will be the emcee for today's auction. I have strict instructions that your phones are to be turned off at all times. We do not want them on silent.'

There was a murmur of laughter from the attendees as some of them realised his name referred to a South Australian wine district.

'Yes, I know. I am Jacobs Kreik from the Barossa Valley in South Australia, and yes, I'm originally from Tanunda. What else would I do but sell wine? Thanks, Mum and Dad.'

Rose whispered to Nic. 'I should introduce him to my mother, Jana Palmer, or as you call her, "Parma-Giana."'

Jacob continued: 'You will have had the opportunity to review the wine available today, and there are many dozens and single bottles to purchase. It is full payment due upon drop of the hammer, and you will not be permitted to take the product unless full payment has been made today. There is a fifteen per cent commission on every sale, per normal auction conditions, and we'll be starting in five minutes. Lord Siimon and Prince Michael have taken your details at the door. Please make a clear bid. The Auctioneer will look for a second confirmation of the bid, and you will have two seconds to confirm. I am also authorised to take bids, along with Lord Siimon and Prince Michael. Any questions?'

A gentleman stood up behind Nic's group. 'Is the owner of this magnificent collection, the Lord Julian Somersby-Kent, in attendance today? I see his son, but the man appears absent from the auction again.'

Lord Siimon took the response. 'I'm sorry Sir, but what are you meaning by 'again'? He was not due to attend this auction here today.'

'Again, as in missing son. He wasn't at the auction recently held in Japan, nor the one previous to that, a month earlier in Dubai.'

'Sir, I believe he could not travel to Japan due to not completing his mandatory vaccines in time. He was, however, in Dubai.'

'I'm sorry, Lord Somersby-Kent. I was in Dubai, and he certainly was not there.'

Siimon added. 'Perhaps you simply missed him. He is a very reclusive man.'

'Not good enough son. Can you please ring him now and see where he is, or at least confirm that he will attend tomorrow's auction?'

Siimon glared at him. 'No sir, I certainly will not. Are you calling into question the integrity of our operations? You have an issue with something. How can I alleviate your concern?'

Nic whispered to Rose. 'That was an interesting comment about Japan as you don't need vaccines to travel there anymore.'

Rose nodded, and Nic continued a little louder, hoping it may be overheard. 'Let's open a bottle at random. One that is for sale here, and let Jacob taste it.'

A bidder sitting directly behind him overheard the comment. 'How about we open a bottle of wine at random, Lord Somersby-Kent, and have Jacob confirm the quality of the contents.'

'I will certainly do that, sir. It will be a pleasure.'

Nic whispered again. 'This will be interesting.'

Sandy then stood up and asked to be dismissed. 'I'm sorry, Lord Siimon, may I take my leave momentarily to use the facilities?'

Lord Siimon glared at Sandy, ignored her question and waited for Sandy to leave the room. He then continued and made a sweeping hand gesture along the wine collection.

'You choose Jacob, any wine out of any box. The cost is irrelevant. We guarantee all our wines and will replace them if spoilt too.'

Jacob nodded and proceeded along the line of bottles available. He stopped at a boxed dozen of 1927 Chateau D'Bourdeilles and selected a single bottle. He then placed the bottle in the vintage brass wine opener secured on the end of the display table and slowly released the cork. Rolling the cork through his fingers, he absorbed the aroma, poured a generous sample into the glass, and offered it to both suspicious men. The first man came up and savoured the wine and they agreed it was indeed a wine from a region of France.

Sandy returned. 'It's a fake Nic.'

'Why?'

'I turned on my phone and googled it when I was in the bathroom. There's no such winery as Chateau D'Bourdeilles. It is a castle, and it is in the south of France, but it never was a winery. Do we do something?'

'Nup, we just won't buy that box of wine. It may just be mislabelled. You can't tell what year a wine is from by the taste, only the region. That takes an expert and these guys won't embarrass themselves by their ignorance.'

Jacob had made his way back to the lectern: 'Thank you, Ladies and Gentlemen. Now that the integrity of the collection has been confirmed let's proceed with the auction. Please let me introduce you to Monsieur Phillipe Megaine. He is from the French wine region of Bordeau, and will be our Auctioneer today.'

There was a small round of applause.

Rose leaned into Nic. 'Do you want me to throw some French at him to see if he is a fake, too?'

Nic shook his head. 'Nup, as we don't know where it will go, and I have to keep things under some control. It's the known and the known unknowns that we need to know. Not the unknown unknowns.'

'Well done. You're back to talking in gobble-de-gook. Great to know, you know.'

'Thanks, Rose.'

The man took centre stage. 'Bonjour, Ladies and Gentlemen. I will not bore you with my history. I am here only to sell you this collection. Is everyone ready? *Laisse procedurer*. Let us proceed.'

The lots were selling quickly, and vigorous bidding surrounded the room. Lord Siimon and Prince Michael quickly accepted the bids.

Nic stood up, then whispered to Rose: 'Bid on the next lot, go up to two thousand if you have to. I'm going closer to the front to look around the room to see where the bids are coming from.' Nic moved off, and Sandy moved into his seat. 'What's going on? Has Nic bid on anything yet?'

'He's going to watch the room.'

The lot Rose was to bid on came up. It quickly rose in $200 increments, then stalled at $1600, so she raised her left hand to her cheek. The Auctioneer saw it and took the bid.

Sandy noticed and whispered, 'Did you just bid?'

Rose ignored her. The bidding was now going up in $50 raises, it stopped again at $1950. Rose bid again by touching her nose.

Sandy whispered again. 'Stop bidding. That was you again, wasn't it.' Rose ignored her once again.

Sandy looked at Nic, who was non-responsive, and then she realised what was happening. Nic was watching Lord Siimon and Prince Michael, who was *not* watching him. The bidding exceeded the $2,000 mark and was heading quickly towards $2,500.

The bidder who previously questioned the collection suddenly stood up. 'Stop this! Stop this! No one is bidding against me. You two at the front are taking bids that don't exist. Lord Siimon, explain yourself.'

'That's not true, Sir. I have a genuine bidder directly in front of me. I would ask that you refrain from further accusations as to the integrity of the process. You are welcome to leave. Jacob, please assist with the removal of this man.'

The disgruntled man moved to the exit. 'I'm going. I'm going. You will hear from my legal representative. This is a scam. The wines are fake, and this auction is a sham.'

Nic smiled and watched as Lord Siimon moved to Jacob and went over to the Auctioneer, who then announced: 'I'm sorry, Ladies and Gentlemen, I have received word from the seller that this auction will stop immediately. The unsold collection here today will be available at tomorrow's auction.'

The auction wound up quickly, and payments were collected from the successful bidders. Rose was not required to purchase her bottle as the sale had been rescinded.

Sandy, Rose and Nic then met with Elvis at the front of the Hotel, and they watched the crowd leave. 'I came in near the end, Mr Nic and looked through the side door, and the angry dude was right. A lot of times, there were not any bidders.'

'Yep, I thought the same thing. Let's talk more in the car, not in here. I'll call Chewy to see if he's got any traction on the mysterious Prince Michael.' Nic moved away to make the call.

Elvis looked over to Rose. 'You were great in there. I couldn't tell you were bidding. No wonder the dude got angry, and he had a partner in there with him, he was sitting on the other side of Sandy.'

Rose nodded. 'Did you work out how much wine was sold in the end?'

Elvis did a quick calculation. 'Yes, it was about ninety-five thousand dollars. The most expensive was that half dozen crate of 1927 Chateau D'Bourdeilles, and the buyer was also given the open bottle. It went for fifteen grand.'

'It's a fake too. Sandy googled the label when she went off to the bathroom. There's no such winery in France or anywhere else in the world.'

'No wonder you have to keep your phones turned off as the buyers would be checking every wine label. Surely they must do their homework?'

'That's part of the scam, Elvis. They insist you don't have access to any information from the start, so you're relying on the seller's integrity unless you have a good memory. I guess it could be the same at an art auction.'

'I expect so, as the bidders just get caught up in the heat of the moment, and if one or two buyers get suspicious, they are quickly removed.'

Nic returned and they stepped into the car and headed to the resort. Sandy piped up from the back seat. 'So, did Chewy find anything?'

Nic nodded. 'Not much. There was a minor hit on the picture of Prince Michael, though. He also has a low social profile, but Chewy tracked him to a flight arrival from Adelaide earlier in the week. With the right connections, getting passenger listings from QANTAS is easy. He searched for Prince Michael of Lyon on the internet.'

Sandy leaned forward. 'I thought access to that was not permitted by law, or it's against QANTAS rules.'

'Technically, it is, but he has his way. I don't know his way or care to know.'

Elvis spoke up. 'Oh, sorry Mr Nic, I got bailed up by Jacob again just before the auction. I might have mentioned that you were here on behalf of the Palmers from Queensland. I assume he took it as the Palmer Group. I didn't care to clarify that it was just "Rose Palmer"'.

'Good job, and I don't think Rose will ever be 'just' a Rose Palmer as she's always going to be more than that.'

'Whoa, Nic. Where did that come from?'

‘Oh, sorry, did I say that out aloud? When I drink too much, I get lazy and the words tumble out even before I think about what I’m saying.’

Rose looked at him. ‘But you’ve only been drinking chai tea.’

CHAPTER 16

They were having dinner in the restaurant at Lookarwi Resort when Lord Siimon approached them with Prince Michael in tow.

'I'm terribly sorry you had to see that today, Lord Crawley. I know Miss Jones, was bidding for you. Can I offer the bottle of wine you were not successful in winning?'

Nic stood up and shook the man's hand. 'I certainly appreciate the gesture. We were willing to go well beyond the two and a half thousand for the bottle. I can't accept it. It is simply too generous.'

'No Sir, my father appreciates your attendance, and I hope it has not tainted tomorrow's auction for you. I believe you are representing the Palmers from Queensland, and thank you again.'

'Yes, we are Lord Somersby-Kent, but it was not supposed to be known. Please keep it a secret. I don't want the prices to escalate unnecessarily during the auction.' The man tapped his nose with his finger, nodded to Prince Michael, and left the bottle on the table.

Sandy began fanning her hands in front of her. 'Cripes Nic, that Prince Michael of Lyon is even better looking close up. I had to hold my breath.' Nic grinned. 'Have you worked out where you know him from yet?'

'Nope, but I'll give my dad a ring later tonight. I sent him the photo, too. It has something to do with Adelaide, but I can't work out what it is. Maybe I'll dream about him. There's something about his pale blue eyes, blonde hair, and extremely good looks.'

Nic pretended to pout as they started to leave the area, then called out. 'Hey, I've got nice eyes, like pools of dark chocolate. Rose said so, isn't that something?'

Rose waved without turning around. 'Aye, Aye.'

It was now nearing eleven p.m., and there was a knock on Nic's door. He rose from his bed, opened it, and Sandy was in her pyjamas. 'Sandy, I um ...maybe you shouldn't be here.'

'Sorry, but I just got off the phone with Dad and I know where Prince Michael is from. We were in the middle of a chat, and Dad was sitting on his front porch having a late whiskey.'

'Is this going somewhere?'

'Yes. We laughed at the fact that every year I get mailed the latest copy of the South Australian Fire Fighters Calendar, and yet they've never personally delivered one. Anyway, Dad said my luck may have finally changed as a Fire Truck came barrelling down his street.'

'And...?'

'I realised that Prince Michael was in one of the calendars. He was Mr September, so I got Dad to get the calendar from his filing cabinet to check.

His name is not Prince Michael of Lyon. It's Michael Prince, and he's even signed his name on the page. I remembered that I'd bought it from him at the Adelaide Show. He's probably here between shifts.'

'Good to know, but you could've told me this in the morning.'

'Or, I could have rung you on the phone, but I was too excited to wait.'

'Thanks, Sandy, and you too, Rose.'

Rose moved out from being around in the corridor. 'How did you know I was here too? Oh, that's right, you know stuff, do stuff and see through walls.'

'See you for breakfast then. We have a big day tomorrow and I think it will all come crashing down around them. Chewy convinced the local constabulary to call on the real Lord Somersby-Kent in their castle. They were home, and were surprised someone had been using their names to sell wines around the world.'

Rose added. 'It's been going on for over twelve months. Surely, they'd seen or heard something?'

'They live 'off-grid', and like many estate owners in the UK, the taxes are killing them, so they don't get out much. Anyway, let's talk more about it tomorrow.'

In the morning, they were having breakfast at the resort, and Jacob approached them. 'Morning Lord Crawley, from Downton Abbey. Are you ready for another day of bidding on the glorious French wines?'

'I don't know about that, Jacob. I'll be there, but we won't be bidding this time. It's a sham, and if you care to ring the real Lord Julian Somersby-Kent in England, he'd be happy to have a chat.'

'What are you talking about, Lord Crawley?'

'Well, for a start, I'm not Lord Crawley. My name is Nic Thorn, and I'm investigating this auction on behalf of the Margaret River Wine Industry Corporation. They've asked me to investigate why an English Lord would auction his wines here as it undermines the local industry. That was just the start, and then my team researched all the bogus wine auctions they've been running.'

Jacob took a step back. 'So, what's your evidence? There will be a lot of disappointed collectors if what you are saying is true. They recently held a wine auction in Tokyo and Dubai, too. That's a big call, Mr Thorn.'

'Well, for a start, let's open this bottle of '82 Chateau Lafayette Rothchild that I was bidding on yesterday, which was generously given to me last night by Lord Siimon, the Faker.'

Nic placed the bottle on the table, removed the wax seal, and uncorked the wine, then poured it into two glass tumblers. 'Bottoms up.'

Jacob looked at him suspiciously, swilled the contents in the glass, held it up, and breathed in the aroma, sipped it and savoured the taste. 'Did you change the contents?'

'Nope, you just saw me unseal the cork.'

'Well, it's French. I would say from Chateau a la Ronce. It tastes and smells like blackberry juice, but I would say it's French blackberry juice.'

Jacob sighed and looked at Nic. 'So, where to from here, the former Lord Crawley?'

Nic smiled. 'Please call me Nic, and Rose and Sandy are my associates. At this stage, it will be business as usual at the auction, but don't be surprised if it suddenly stops.'

Jacob nodded. 'Thanks, Nic, but I'm unsure what to do now. I've got to tell the buyers and get this thing cancelled.'

'Not yet, please leave it to me. We can't let them know what we're up to. Besides, we have to find the elusive Lord Julian the Faker. I've got an idea where he is, but I'm not sure how we bring him out into the open. We'll see you at the auction tomorrow, Jacob.'

Jacob took a deep breath and left the resort a little slower than he had arrived.

Rose watched him leave. 'Do you think he'll let the cat out of the bag?'

'Nup. He's got his reputation to worry about. As long as we stop it today, he'll be happy, I hope.'

'So, where's the elusive Lord Julian the Faker then? I assume it wasn't on the yacht, so it must be at the warehouse that Elvis suggested, then?'

'Yep, but I'm unsure how we can get to him or take down Lord Siimon, the Scammer and Sandy's beau-to-be, Michael, the former Fireman. I'll have to think about it.'

Elvis entered the breakfast area and sat down with them. 'I just saw Jacob in the carpark. He looked destroyed. Did something happen, Mr Nic?'

'Yep, I just filled him in on the wine auction scam. Chewy found out that he'd also allowed Lord Julian the Faker to borrow money against the wine collection. Looks like he's in for about two hundred and fifty thousand dollars.'

Sandy piped up. 'Can you use wine as security for a loan? That's dumb. What if you drink it?'

Nic nodded. 'Not really, as they store the bottles elsewhere. Any pawnbroker will take anything as security as long as you intend to pay the loan back. If you don't, they own the asset and can sell it to recover their losses.'

Sandy shook her head. 'So, how much wine would he have put up?'

'Well, it would depend on the integrity of the collection, but if Jacob has fully maxed it out, he may have taken the full value. If they become valueless, he will be feeling a little sick by now.'

Elvis nodded. 'I would say that's how he was looking, and he was staring at his phone.'

'OK, let's get dressed for the show and arrive early. We'll see what Lord Siimon and Prince

Michael get up to this time. I doubt Lord Julian will turn up though.'

'Give us an hour to get ready, and we'll see you back in the foyer at ten.'

'FAB.'

Rose, Sandy and Elvis were waiting in the foyer. It was now after ten, and it was very unlike Nic to keep them waiting. 'I bet he's had another nana-nap. Should we go and wake him?'

'Nope, here he comes now.' This came from Elvis, and Rose and Sandy looked at Nic and laughed. 'What's the joke guys? Were you laughing at me?'

'Not everything is about you. Sometimes it's about us. How come you're late?'

'I was talking through this thing with Chewy, and we've come up with an idea. You might be getting a little damp Sandy.'

Rose groaned. 'Damn you, Nic. Hang on, why Sandy and not me?'

Nic grinned. 'You'll see, Rose.'

They drove to the Margaret River Hotel for the auction where Lord Siimon and Prince Michael welcomed everyone upon entry. Details were collected at the door, phones were required to be turned off, and as each person entered, they were handed a glass of red wine.

Lord Siimon closed the doors behind him and went to the front of the room: 'Thank you for your attendance today. All the wines that we are presenting today are also offered for tasting. For those of you at yesterday's auction, some of our clients were suspicious of the product. Enjoy.'

Jacob came over to Nic. 'That's very clever of them, Nic, as it's the genuine article we are tasting.' Nic softly nodded. 'I don't doubt it, Jacob. Are you still OK with this?'

'I'm not exactly OK, but I've checked you out. I wish you'd told me sooner.'

'I couldn't Jacob. We didn't know how big this was. My crew managed to get on board the yacht and found a picture of the real Lord Julian Somersby-Kent. We did facial recognition on the portrait, then searched the internet and found the match.'

Jacob sighed. 'When did you know it was a scam?'

'It was not until early this morning, but I had my suspicions. When the disgruntled dude raised the issue about the Dubai auction, and Lord Si-imon was adamant that Lord Julian was there, we ran through all the visions available. Though it was only a few frames, it was just enough for us to find the fake Lord Julian.'

'He won't be here today though, will he? How will you catch him?'

'Leave it with me. I will say that the auction may start, but something will go down before the first bid is taken. Just work with us. Please don't overplay anything. I'll work hard to recover the money you are in for, too.'

'Oh, you know about that too?'

'Yep, I assume it's the full ante? Did he leave the full two hundred and fifty grand worth of wine against the loan?'

'Actually, it's over two hundred thousand. He said he was going to leave anything left unsold at the auctions for the balance. That's why I wasn't too concerned when yesterday's auction stalled.'

'OK, just remember to keep breathing, and we'll get through this.'

The auctioneer called everyone to take their seats. 'Please ensure you are registered and have your bidding paddles ready. It will be a frenzy here today. You have been savouring the wines. You know the product, and you've seen the collection. We will start in around ten minutes.'

Nic showed Rose to her seat. 'Please hold the two seats for Sandy and me as we've got something to do. If you hear me calling out, get to us ASAP.'

Rose nodded. 'Where will you be?'

'Close, but remember others in play might not be part of our team.' Nic and Sandy moved away and went through the two-way door into the kitchen area. Rose was watching Lord Siimon and Prince Michael at the front of the room when their helicopter pilot approached them. 'Excuse me, Lord Siimon. I should clear out these empty bottles. Do you mind if I do?'

Lord Siimon glared at him. 'Get them out of the way, and what've I told you about speaking to us?'

The pilot nodded, collected the wooden crates of bottles, and headed towards the same two-way door Nic and Sandy had just walked through.

The man, however, was walking backwards, and as his hands were full, he leaned his back into the door, and it opened behind him by someone unseen. As he had expected some resistance from the closed door, he stumbled backwards and crashed onto the kitchen floor. The swinging door closed as he fell backwards, and there was the sound of smashing glass.

A woman screamed, and Rose recognised it was Sandy. Some people in the room, having seen what had happened, gasped loudly. A voice then came from beyond the closed door. 'I'm so sorry. I didn't realise he was at the door. He's bleeding, he's bleeding.'

Nic swung open the doors and leant out: 'Is there a Doctor or nurse here? Quickly, someone, please call an ambulance.'

Rose took her prompt and stood up. 'I'm an ICU Nurse. Get some towels and a cold compress to stop the bleeding. How bad is it?'

Sandy then came through the door carrying two halves of smashed bottles. The edges were jagged, and the front of her dress was covered in a dark red stain.

'It's in his back; the rest of the broken bottles are stuck in his back. It's black blood....it's bad...very bad.'

Suddenly, there was a call out from a woman within the crowd. 'I'm a retired Doctor; please let me through. Black blood is not good. Let me through.'

Rose and the Doctor went through the door, then she leaned down to attend to the prostrate man.

Nic whispered to the Doctor. 'Hi, my name is Nic Thorn, and I am here investigating a suspected wine auction fraud. We need a favour before you start. Firstly, I must tell you that this wine auction is part of a worldwide scam.'

The Doctor looked at him suspiciously, and Nic continued: 'Can you please read this aloud?'

The Doctor hesitated. 'But I need to check him.'

'I understand, but first, please read this aloud.'

'I... he won't die on my watch. I've never lost a patient in forty years of practice.'

'That's fine Doc. I promise you won't lose this one either.' Nic held the note to the Doctor, and she read it aloud: 'It's the femoral artery... he is losing much blood. I can't stop the bleeding. Cuts are too deep!' The Doctor looked at Nic again. 'What is this all about? I don't like it.'

Meanwhile, Sandy was standing on the room side of the door, preventing anyone else from coming in, and Nic put his finger to his mouth.

'Please wait a second; then I need you to read something else.' The Doctor leaned down to the patient, took hold of the unconscious man's wrist, and felt for a pulse. 'This pulse is strong.'

'Yes, it is. We needed a distraction to shake things up at the wine auction. Now, please read this aloud, too.'

The Doctor reluctantly obliged and read aloud: 'We need an immediate evacuation. Can anyone fly a helicopter? I saw one in the estate. This man needs to get to Fremantle Hospital stat.'

As Sandy was out in the main room, she called out. 'Elvis. Our man Elvis. He's a helicopter pilot. He can fly it. He can fly it.'

Lord Siimon looked towards Elvis. 'Is that true? Can you fly a Robinson chopper?'

Elvis nodded. 'Yes, but we'll need to make space in the back for a stretcher. We'll need to remove the wine crates.'

Lord Siimon looked at him. 'Yes. OK, let's do it. You can fly my helicopter to the hospital. Prince Michael, you stay here. We'll have to cancel the auction until I return.' He turned to the gathered crowd. 'I'm sorry, Ladies and Gentlemen, the auction will have to wait.'

Meantime, Nic began explaining the wine scam to the Doctor. 'We didn't expect you to get involved. That's why we had a script ready, just in case.'

The Doctor was still considering her position. 'OK, I'll continue to help you with the charade, but I want to know more when it's over.' They wrapped the injured man in a sheet and towels, and Nic looked down at the makeshift bandaging. The Doctor wiped her bloodied hands on a cloth and smelled the red stain.

'I'm sorry Mr Thorn. I don't suffer fools gladly. Is this man injured? Is he going to the hospital?' This doesn't smell like blood.'

'That's a no and a yes, and a no, but we still have to get him to the helicopter and into Fremantle. We must keep up the illusion that he's still bleeding profusely, but we weren't expecting anyone else to get involved. We planned to use Rose as an ICU Nurse.'

The Doctor looked over at Rose. 'Are you really an ICU Nurse, young lady?'

Rose shook her head. 'Nope.'

The Doctor continued. 'OK, OK...I think I understand, but I'll still want more explanation before you leave.'

Nic nodded. 'Done, Doc. Now let's get him out to the helicopter.'

The Doctor, Nic, Rose and Elvis carried the victim and carefully placed him into the helicopter. Lord Siimon and Prince Michael had removed the wine crates and placed them away from the helicopter pad.

Elvis climbed in, and Lord Siimon entered from the other side. They donned headphones and were soon airborne.

Nic smiled as they watched it rise, and then he whispered to the Doctor. 'Do you fancy a Penfolds' Grange Hermitage?'

Doc sighed. 'I do, Mr Thorn, but I'll still check you out with some of my people.'

Nic smiled. 'Thanks again for what you've done. In my line of work, we can't predict how everyone will react. It's the known unknowns that we know might need to know, you know.'

Doc nodded. 'Do you often talk in gobble-de-gook, Mr Thorn?' Rose overheard. 'That he does, Doc.'

Meantime, Prince Michael was watching the chopper fly from view, and Sandy walked up to him holding a coloured sheet of paper rolled into a scroll. 'Hi Prince Michael of Lyon, my name is Sandy. Would you like to sign this?'

The man looked at her, smiled, and unfurled the paper. It was his picture from the South Australian Firefighters Calendar. '...Where did you get this?'

Sandy smiled. 'It is you, Michael Prince. It was your blue eyes. You signed the calendar for me at the Adelaide Show a couple of years ago. Have you had the flame tattoos removed? The ones on your forearms?'

Prince Michael grabbed at his sleeves, but Nic was quicker and had already undone the cufflinks to enable the sleeves to be rolled up. The tattoos were still there. He looked around for an escape route or an ally, but nothing was forthcoming, so he stood there shaking his head.

'You stupid woman, stupid Firefighters Calendar, stupid, stupid. What am I going to do now? I can't go back to Adelaide. They fired me.'

Nic looked at him. 'That's funny, you got fired from the Fire Brigade. You could always go into stand-up comedy.'

Representatives from the Margaret River Wine Industry Corporation appeared along with the Police and secured his arrest.

The Doctor ventured to the huddle to further validate all that had just happened, then turned to Nic. 'I think I'll take at least three bottles of The Grange. I must admit it's all very clever of you, and I like it.'

Nic nodded. 'Well, Doc, it's not over yet.'

he Doctor and Nic returned to the kitchen and Rose was busy with a bucket and mop. 'This fake blood stuff is sticky, Nicky, and it's tricky to mop up.' Nic picked up the two wooden crates of unbroken empty wine bottles and moved them out of the way.

The Doctor looked at them, then at Nic. 'So what was the smash then? Those aren't broken?'

'It was all part of the ruse. We set up a mattress, and the pilot fell onto that.'

The Doctor looked around. 'But all the blood? It looked so real.'

Rose showed her the plastic bottles of sauce. 'The dark blood is blackberry syrup, and the red is a mix of tomato and hickory sauce.'

The Doc smiled. 'Please select three bottles from the 2012 Penfolds Grange: one to drink and two to store. I like what your team have done here. Please let me know if I can help with anything else.' The Doc then headed off to join her party.

CHAPTER 17

Meantime, Elvis was flying the helicopter and they were almost into Fremantle. Lord Siimon was not talking, just staring out the window. The injured man lying prostrate in the rear was starting to moan again, and Lord Siimon pointed to the foreground.

'There's already a Helicopter on the Hospital helipad, Elvis, so we won't be able to land there.'

'No, I've got to look for somewhere else. Somewhere close.'

The man stirred from the rear. 'There's a field by the old jail. I've used it before. There, go there.....'

'Roger that.'

Elvis gently banked the helicopter and headed further north from the Hospital landing area. 'It looks like we've got a welcoming committee.'

There were red and blue flashing lights of an Ambulance and Police cars below them. Lord Siimon nodded down at them. 'Good. At least they know we're coming.'

Elvis brought the chopper to a soft landing, and the two policemen made their way up to the pad once the blades stopped rotating. Lord Siimon noticed that the two Ambulance Officers had not yet moved. 'What's going on? Why aren't the Ambulance Officers here first?'

The victim in the chopper sat up and peeled off the bandages. 'Oh, the two Detectives are here for you, Lord, Siimon. I'm fine now, too. Thanks for asking.'

Lord Siimon turned around and glared at him.

Elvis then jumped out, and the lead Detective leaned into the space: 'Good afternoon, Lord Siimon, or whoever you are. You are under arrest for wine fraud.'

Less than a kilometre away, another man was in a warehouse, un-corking wine bottles, emptying them and re-filling them with wine from large plastic tubs. He was listening to a song made famous by English band UB40's from the '80s, 'Red, red wine...goes to my head...' and smiled at the irony.

He glanced down at his phone, and as it was now 4 p.m., his expected call was late, so he was getting a little anxious. The man decided to stop what he was doing, collected his phone, slid open the warehouse door and stepped into the afternoon sunshine.

After working inside for six hours, the warm sun felt good on his face. so he pulled his Rosewood pipe from his pocket, tapped it on the heel of his shoe, stuffed it in the tobacco and lit it. The familiar sound of a helicopter pulled him from his reverie, and he watched as it flew overhead. It made a turn, began hovering above him, and then his phone rang. 'This is Julian Somersby-Kent. How may I assist you?'

There was no response. 'Hello, are you there, Si-imon?'

'Sorry, Lord Julian. My name is Lord Crawley of Highclere Castle. Siimon is otherwise occupied. He told me to let you know that everything went as planned, and he managed to dispose of all the stock.'

'I'm sorry, Sir, I do not know whom you think you are, but you certainly cannot be Lord Crawley of Highclere Castle. That is where they film Downton Abbey, and Crawley is the name made up by Julian Cleary for the TV show.'

'Oh, I must be mistaken. I cannot be Lord Crawley, nor can you be the real Lord Julian Somersby-Kent.' The man went silent, so Nic continued: 'Oh, by the way, the helicopter rental hire is overdue, and that might explain why it's hovering above you.'

'My young man, you certainly take liberties with your statements. You have no idea who I am or how long I have been doing this.'

'Well, it's like this, Terrence Timothy Thomas-Tollen of Tewkesbury. Did all those 'T's in your name make you leave Mother England for a better time of scamming wine collectors?'

The man moved back inside and disconnected the call, he then rang Siimon's number, and again, Nic answered: 'Hello, Terry. This is Lord Voldemort; how can I help you?'

The man shut the call down and dialled Prince Michael's number. Nic answered again: 'Hello, Terry. It's me. I'm the Lord Almighty, and your numbers are up this time.'

The man dropped his phone on the ground and stomped on it, smashing it to pieces. He then noticed the familiar red and blue flashing hues from Police cars entering the warehouse carpark, then looked around at his work site and realised there was too much incriminating evidence to destroy.

There was a loud knock on the warehouse door: *'Open up. This is Detective Alison Moore, and we have a warrant for your arrest, Mr Thomas-Tollen.'*

The man slid open the door, then recognised Jacob from the Auction House, but not the man standing with two women.

One of the women had a dark red stain on her dress. The man approached Jacob. 'I think there has been a misunderstanding here, Jacob. I believe I am owed an apology by someone pretending to be Lord Crawley from Downton Abbey.'

Jacob nodded and put his left hand onto the man's shoulder, but his right hand was balled into a fist. Jacob threw the punch which caught him directly in the face.

Terrence slumped to the ground, shaking his head, and the younger man stood over him. 'I've lost a lot of money from your wine auction scam, and my people aren't happy.'

Terrence looked up at him, wiped his bloodied nose with his sleeve and muttered, 'Oh, stop your whining.'

The police placed him in handcuffs and led him to the back of the police wagon to join Siimon and Michael. They looked at each other and said nothing.

Nic and his group then entered the warehouse. There were at least five one-thousand-litre Fermentation Tanks, and three were half-empty.

Jacob quickly counted the bottles and rounded them off to a thousand, and as they went further through the site, located an overflowing bucket of corks and a bucket of warm red wax for re-capping the bottles.

'How was he going to sell all this, Mr Thorn?'

'My guy found out that after being here in Western Australia, he'd organised a delivery of wine to the Rhine District of Germany. He was on the move again and needed to find a ship to take the product, relocate and start over again. Interpol was onto him, but we got there first.'

Sandy looked at the pile of labels on one of the tables. 'He's printing his labels here too. He might be involved with those scammers in Cambodia and the 'Benfolds' thing?'

'Yep, I'd say so.'

Jacob looked at the labels, then around at all the wine. 'So how do I recover my losses, Mr Thorn? Any wine bottles that have been opened are valueless and the opened bottles couldn't be sold. I assume everything here will be destroyed or kept as evidence until this goes to court?'

'Probably, but I assume you would've registered a Property Security Charge over all the Lord's company's assets when you took the wine as collateral. So, you have a legal right to retain all of this, which includes the Fermentation Tanks as recovered items.'

Jacob nodded. 'Yes, we do that as part of the loan process, but this uncorked wine is worthless, and the used tanks don't sell for much.'

'You're right, but you forget it would include all of the Lord's collection. My guys have found a storage Unit at Tullamarine Airport in Melbourne registered to Terrence Thomas-Tollen. All you need to do is prove that they are the same person and that you have a valid contract with him, you'll be entitled to the ownership of the contents of the storage unit.'

'Are your guys good enough to know what's stored in them?'

'Sort of, as he's insured the unit for about five hundred thousand dollars.'

'Thanks, Mr Thorn.'

Jacob moved away with a bit of spring in his step, and the Police Investigation Team began dismantling the warehouse.

Nic, Rose and Sandy returned to Elvis and the car. 'So Mr Nic, where to now?'

Nic nodded. 'Head back to the resort, where we'll stay overnight, then return to Perth for a flight to Adelaide.'

Elvis smiled. 'Are you taking Sandy home for a well-earned break?'

'Not exactly as we're off to have a serious look into budgie smugglers.'

The following afternoon, Nic's group was waiting in the QANTAS Lounge in Perth, and Elvis was trying to work out if he could spare the time to join them in Adelaide.

'Hey Mr Nic, are you sure you couldn't use a chopper pilot where you are going? I get the need to fly and drive, but Rose keeps reminding me that she doesn't like the little planes you tend to fly. You could use a helicopter.'

'Sorry, mate. I have a vision of a rising flock of budgerigars trying to avoid helicopter blades. I can't see that working out.'

'I'm always available if you can get to the west again. Make it real soon, as I miss the Nic Thorn excitement.'

'No worries. By the way, I've spoken to the Rottnest Island Tourist people, and they want to re-introduce the helicopter flights. If you can convince your pilot mate, I reckon you've got a new business venture waiting for you.'

'Thanks, Mr Nic, and I loved working with your two friends, too. You've got a great team. Did you set up the nurse and Doctor thing with Rose, or was that all planned?'

Rose looked at him. 'No, Nic only told me to be ready for something, then the real Doctor joined in. I nursed it from there.'

'You guys are really good together, and maybe you might get to work with Nic's sister too. Say hello to her from me when you do.'

Rose and Sandy looked at Nic, and he shook his head. 'Never going to happen, guys.'

Flight QF555 is now boarding for Adelaide.

They stood up and said their final goodbyes and Elvis did his best Elvis Presley hip wiggle, then the classic static stance, and waved them off. 'Elvis has left the building, and until next time, Ah-ha-hum.'

CHAPTER 18

Rose and Sandy had taken their seats in Business Class and watched as Nic made his way down the plane's rear, where he met with a Flight Attendant, and there was a deep discussion.

Finally, Nic shook his head, turned around, and returned to Business Class. He sat down in the chair directly behind Rose and Sandy, but this time, someone was in the other seat.

It was the Doctor from Margaret River Hotel. Nic nodded and shook her hand. 'So Nic Thorn, I've checked you out. You've got quite a reputation with the top end of town, haven't you? They wouldn't give much away, something about maintaining a low profile?'

Nic said nothing, and the Doc continued: 'Are you flying off to your next wine scam? Is this one in the Barossa Valley, just outside Adelaide?'

'This time, it's bird smuggling. We are flying to Broken Hill on Monday with the Royal Flying Doctor Service, then driving back over the border to Boolcoomatta Reserve. Do you know it?'

'Yes. Now that I'm retired, I have the time for twitching. I wish my husband were still here to enjoy it with me, though. Sadly, I lost him a year ago. I was in Perth visiting my son, Kathy, and my grandchildren.'

The Doc smiled and continued. 'Was everything you did pretend?' Nic shrugged.

Rose called out. 'So Nic, Captain James T. Kirk is not flying this one?'

The Doctor responded instead. 'My son told me about that. He'd said he was the Captain of the Enterprise. That was you?'

Sandy piped up this time. 'I knew straight away he was one of Nic's mates.' The Doctor laughed and looked at Rose. 'And now you get to fly with me, Miss Palmer.'

'Only to Adelaide, though.'

'Nope, it will be to Broken Hill too. I'm the pilot for the R.F.D.S.'

Nic grinned. 'I think I'll be handing over a couple more Penfolds Grange then.'

'Well, it's time I formally introduce myself to you, Mr Thorn. I'm Doctor Vanesa Haylen, retired, but please keep calling me Doc as everyone else does.'

About three hours later, they landed in Adelaide, and Rose leaned around from her chair. 'Hey Doc, please wake up grumpy from being sleepy. Can you ask Nic if his driver is picking us up and where we are staying?'

Nic responded. 'I'm awake, Snow White, and yes, Driver is organised, but I've forgotten where you're staying. I'll be at my apartment in East End, and you two will be...um...'

Rose scoffed at the comment. 'That's so typical of you, now that you're nearly forty, you've forgotten about your associates.'

The Doctor laughed. 'There are plenty of quality hotels you could put up in, but not much up East End Adelaide way. Over near Government House, you've got the Stamford and the Intercontinental, and there are many new boutique ones around now, too.'

Rose smiled. 'Oh, we can't do the Stamford. Nic stayed there once, and we still have to return to apologise.'

'That's not true, Doc.'

'Yes, it is, and you got caught with an unnamed woman in your room.'

'C'mon guys. That was my sister. Can't you stop with all of that yet?' Sandy added. 'Nope. Not until you tell us her name so when we finally meet, we'll know what to call her.'

Sandy and Rose looked at each other and were the first to disembark, so they waited for Nic. 'Damn, we've left sunny Perth to land in sunny Adelaide, and the sun's almost gone to bed already.'

Nic approached. 'Yep, and we've got a few days before we head off to Broken Hill with Doc in the little red R.F.D.S. plane.'

Rose sighed. 'Sandy wants to catch up with her Father. Is there anything else you want us to do?'

'Nup, but we might need to study up on birds. I'm a twitcher from way back.'

They disembarked and moved into the luggage collection area, where Nic's driver was waiting for them. The man was dressed in a tracksuit with a whistle around his neck. 'Heya Nic. Sorry, I've been coaching my boys' Under Ten soccer team and lost track of time.'

Nic nodded. 'It's all good. Thanks for coming.'

They collected the luggage, and moved out to the carpark, then stepped into a seven-seater black Mercedes Benz.

A young boy was playing on his iPad in the front.' Driver nodded. 'Welcome back to Adelaide. I've had to swap the car for this Dad's Soccer Taxi. This is my son, Bussie. Please say hello to Mr Thorn, Miss Fraser and Miss Palmer.' The boy nodded hello at each of them. 'Call me Bus.'

Sandy looked at him. 'Your name is Bus Driver?'

'Yes, pretty cool hey. It's my first three initials, B.U.S.'

Nic grinned. 'We don't need to know any more than that little dude. So, Driver, are you still good to fly with us to Broken Hill?'

'Err, about that I ...um.... my boys' team are in the finals next week. I didn't think we had a chance, but two other teams had forfeited. One of the boys came down with whooping cough, so our team is into the Grand Final.'

Bus shrugged, then looked over at his father. 'You haven't told them about your new lady friend yet, Dad.' Driver sighed. 'We've only been in the car five minutes and not even out of the airport.'

Sandy looked at him. 'C'mon then, Driver, spill it. Who is she, and will we get to meet her?'

Driver continued. 'Well, it's only early days. Her name's Charita and she's from Sri Lanka. She spoils the boy and me.'

Nic smiled. 'Nice to hear, Driver.'

Driver grinned. 'Thanks, Nic. Rita's got a great job, too. She does the gas meter readings, so I get to walk with her when she does her rounds. It keeps me trim for the soccer coaching stuff.'

Nic looked at him. 'Rita, is a meter maid?'

'Yep, and she's lovely too.' Driver hesitated. 'I know where you're heading.'

Rose joined in. 'Where are we heading? Are you taking us to our Hotel?'

'Not quite yet Rose. Nic is referring to "Lovely Rita," It's a Beatles song from their Sergeant Peppers Lonely Heart Band Album in '67.'

Bus turned to face them. 'Sergeant Peppers is my favourite record. I like their earlier stuff too when they played in Hamburgers.'

'It was Hamburg, Bus, in Germany, not Hamburgers.'

'Sorry, Dad.'

They were now driving through the Adelaide CBD, and Driver turned right off Grenfell Street, then into Bent Street and stopped before the Majestic Hotel. Nic helped Rose and Sandy from the car. 'I'm sorry guys, it's not the Stamford or Intercontinental, but it's close to my apartment. It's about a ten-minute walk.'

'Why can't we stay at your place?'

'I only have two bedrooms and one bathroom. Nic Thorn doesn't share his bathroom with anyone.'

'You're doing it again, Nic?'

'What? Being selfish?'

Rose sighed. 'No, talking about yourself in the third person.'

Nic shrugged, organised the rooms, and Driver then drove to Nic's East Terrace apartment. 'Where are Dad and I staying, Mr Thorn?'

'I've got the key to the place next door to my apartment. It's just being renovated at the moment, so it might be a bit rough.'

They took the elevator to the second floor, and Nic led them along the corridor to the apartments. 'You guys are in this one, and I'm next door.'

Nic opened the door and showed them in. There were half-plastered walls, the kitchen was incomplete, and the carpet had been rolled up, exposing the concrete. 'I'll put you both in the main bedroom if that's OK. The water and electricity are still on, but you might get a little dusty sleeping on the rolled-up carpet.'

'No worries, I wasn't keen on driving home to Victor Harbour tonight anyway.'

Bus nodded. 'Thank you, Mr Thorn. I'm sure it will be more comfortable here than with the possums in the park.' Driver smiled. 'Bus and I are leaving for Victor before breakfast. Is that still OK?'

'Yep.'

In the morning, Nic texted Rose the address of his apartment, and they arrived shortly after. He led them upstairs to the units and opened the door of the second apartment. 'So what do you think?'

Rose peered in. 'Well, what are we supposed to be looking at? It's a dump. It needs a lot of work and looks like a troll has been living here. Is it your place?'

'Wow, Rose. Why are you so nasty to me so early in the morning? Sandy likes it already, don't you?'

Sandy nodded, 'If you like living in a shoe box, with a view across the park and above a pub in the East End of Adelaide. With a lick of paint, it might just sell.'

Nic nodded. 'Welcome to your next project then.'

'Whose place is it?'

'It belongs to my sister.'

'We'll have a look, but only because we get to discuss the renovations and styling with your sister, and not you.'

'You're on. Do you want to see her now? She's in town.'

Rose looked at him. 'What? No way. What about privacy and protection? It's all about keeping your people safe.'

'Nup, it's all good. We can call her right now.'

Nic set up his iPad on the workbench in the kitchen and connected to the Zoom link. It was answered quickly, and Rose and Sandy held their breath in anticipation at the thought of seeing Nic's sister. When the vision came up, it was very dark, and the person was silhouetted in shadow.

'Hiya, sis, the others are with me, and we're ready to talk about the renovations.'

A message read across the bottom of the screen: '*All good, Bro.*'

Rose leaned forward. 'We can't see her, and the picture is terrible. Where is she?'

'Not here.'

'Damn you, Nic. You said she was in town.'

'Well, she is in a town, but the reception is not so good where she is.'

The very recognisable sound of the three horns from a reversing ferry boat sounded loudly through the speakers, and another statement appeared on the bottom of the screen:

'*What do you need to know?*'

Rose leaned towards the screen. 'Well, firstly, why is the picture so bad? We can't see you at all.'

'*You guys look good, though. Thanks for looking after Nic, too.*'

'From what?... Err ...What do we call you? Nic's never told us your name.'

'*It's Nic.*'

They looked to Nic for a response, and he shrugged. 'Nicole. That's her name, guys. Nic for short.'

Rose shook her head. 'If we call you Nic and your two sisters are also called Nic...you can both get nicked.' Nic shrugged.

Rose and Sandy went through the plans and details of the renovations, the budget and the time-frame, then they disconnected the call, and Nic nodded. 'That went well, didn't it?'

Rose looked at him. 'We didn't even hear what she sounds like, but at least she can type quickly.'

'Yep, she's a fast typist.'

Rose sighed. 'And she wasn't very animated. We didn't even see her hands moving when she was supposed to be typing or replying to us. Most people talk with their hands even on a Zoom call.'

'Yep, you could say that she wasn't bored, though.' Rose added. 'That was a cardboard cut-out, wasn't it?'

Nic shrugged again. 'I thought the Sydney ferry horn sounding out in the background might have given it away.'

Sandy interjected. 'Your sister lives in Murrayville, Victoria, and that's nowhere near Sydney.'

'True, but that wasn't my twin sister. It's the other one. She lives in the beach suburb of Manly, and she was in the town of Sydney.'

'You've got two sisters? You never told us, so does that make you the baby?'

'Nup. I was born two minutes before my twin sister, then Nicole came along a couple of years later.'

Rose grinned. 'So, you're the eldest, which explains a lot.'

'Thanks, I think.'

CHAPTER 19

They were finishing a late breakfast at The Rose café on East Terrace and talking about how much money Nic had made recently.

Nic sighed. 'It's ugly to talk about money, especially mine.'

Rose looked at him. 'You know if we're going to spend your money on the renovations, we need to know that you're good for it.'

'OK, what do you want to know?'

'Well, when we solved Adelaide invoice caper, you said they recovered over a million dollars in the fraudster's bank accounts. Did you get a share of that?'

'Yep.'

'And when you sold your house in Brookwater, Brisbane, did you get all the money?'

'Yep.'

'And any other capers that we've solved, have all the people paid you for them?'

'Yep. So, I'm good for it then?'

Sandy looked at him. 'Nup, not until you tell us your two sisters' real names.'

'It's never going to happen.'

A white Toyota Land Cruiser pulled out the front, and Nic looked up. 'Our ride is here.' He stood up, handed the money over to the cashier and ushered Rose and Sandy toward the car. They stepped in and noticed Doc was driving.

Sandy looked at her. 'What's happened to Driver...our other, other driver?'

Nic nodded. 'He's got Soccer Dad duties. Besides, the Doc needs to get us up to speed on twitching and bird spotting. As well as being our driver, she's also the R.F.D.S. pilot, a twitcher and our guide at the bird sanctuary in two days.'

Doc nodded to Rose and Sandy. 'It's nice to see you again too. We're heading up to my place at Bellevue Heights where I'll make my presentation, and there'll be a test afterwards.'

Rose looked at her. 'You're kidding right?'

'Nope. I do live in Bellevue Heights, so that part is true, but the rest of the talk is up to my four brooding birds.'

Nic nodded. 'We've got about two days to get through the birdy stuff, then we get our own wings and fly up to Broken Hill.'

Doc continued. 'The South Australian Bird Twitching Club is pretty casual, so there's no need to learn too much about the stuff. Any new members are welcome, as it's just an excuse to camp out under the stars and drink red wine. We'll play a bit of music around a campfire, sing a bit, laugh a lot, drink a lot, and look for things that flap. Re-set, and re-start for the next day.'

They were heading southwards out of the city, and the Doc pulled into a carpark at the Mitcham

Shopping Centre. 'Firstly, let's have lunch. Welcome to the Torrens Arms Hotel. It's my local.'

Rose looked at her. 'Sory Doc, we've just had breakfast.'

'That's OK. How about Mr Handsome and I go into the pub, so he can fill me in on what's happening? You two head into the shopping centre. There's a new Kathmandu clothing store, and you'll need to get some warm clothes. Ask for Annie, and she'll kit you in the latest twitching, birdy, camouflagey stuff.'

Rose sighed. 'So, it's now Mr Handsome? Is that your name for this investigation and when do we get special names?'

Nic nodded. 'Yep. I think it's a good name and suits me rather well. I should have thought of it before. The Doc and I will go into the pub and talk about stuff.'

Nic ignored Rose's comments regarding their 'special names'. Rose continued. 'OK, no special names, but what type of stuff?'

The Doc looked at Rose. 'Boy, you ask a lot of questions.'

The group parted ways, and Nic and Doc went into the pub. 'Too early for a whiskey?'

Doc grinned. 'Certainly not. Johnny Walker Red is my poison, and it's just past noon anyway. Tell me what this is all about.'

They found a booth, sat down and Nic considered what Doc would have discovered about his past. 'I'm a Freelance Investigator. I previously worked for the Australian Securities Investigation Organisation, but that's another story for another day. I hooked up with Sandy and Rose about twelve months ago, and we've been running around Australia looking into scams, frauds and genuine misunderstandings. I've been doing this for about ten years, mostly alone. I have a support team in most cities, like Elvis, the helicopter pilot, and my computer geek support guy is based in Melbourne.'

Doc nodded. 'What's the angle with Rose and Sandy?'

'No angle. I like working with them.'

'Are they ex-Army or anything like that? Are they licenced to carry?'

'Nup, they used to run a boutique clothing store in Brisbane. We all live there, although Sandy's father lives here in Adelaide.'

'So, what happens when you get into a fight or something? Do they come to rescue you with their matching handbags and Manolo Blahnik's?'

'Not quite. They are often the diversion. I do my stuff over here whilst everyone is watching them. It is simple and works. No guns, no violence and no one getting hurt, only pride when the scammers realise we've duped them.'

Doc nodded. 'So, I have to fly you to Broken Hill. You do your thing at the bird sanctuary, and then we return home?'

'Yep, that's about it. Have you had any new members that you feel are not quite who they seem?'

'Not really, but we can call the President and have a chat with him if you like.'

'No, that's OK. We'll deal with it when we get there. Although when new members join, do you take ID or anything from them?'

'Nope. It's just an online application. We get their date of birth, address, email and details. I suppose it could be dodgy, but why bother?'

'Well, Doc, it gives them access to all the sites where the rarer birds are. So if they want to meet their supply and demand, you've led them straight there.'

'Gee Nic, you've got a suspicious mind?'

Nic nodded. 'Yep, and I just used it to close down that wine scam in Margaret River. Let's get moving as Rose and Sandy have returned. I almost didn't recognise them in their matching camouflaged outfits.'

They climbed back into the Land Cruiser and Rose held up the receipt. 'Do you want to see this?' Nic shrugged. 'Please file it in the WPB as usual.'

Doc looked over. 'You don't need to keep paper receipts as there's an app on the iPhones that does that. We use it for the Bird Club.'

Nic smiled. 'I file them in the Waste Paper Basket. I don't do paperwork.'

They arrived at Doc's place twenty minutes later, and she drove straight under the house. A DeLorean was parked in the basement garage, along with two Mini Minors, one blue and one red, and a white Lotus Esprit.

Doc nodded over to the cars. 'The Minis are replicas from the '69 Italian Job, that's the good one with Michael Caine. The Lotus is a replica from the '77 James Bond film, and the DeLorean is my time machine.'

Rose looked at the Doc. 'Does it still work?'

'Nope, sorry Rose, the Flux Capacitor has a flat-tery battery.'

Nic looked at the Minis and uttered the classic quote from the movie in his best Michael Caine accent. 'You're only supposed to blow the bloody doors off.'

Rose shook her head, then added a comment in her best Michael Caine accent. 'Hey Nic, I wouldn't presume to tell you what to do with your past; just know that there are those who care about what you do with your future.'

Nic looked at her. 'Wow, you just quoted Alfred from The Batman movie.'

'Yes, I did. I listen to what you tell me I should know to keep us safe, but watching Batman, the super-hero who has no super-hero powers, that's something I struggle with.'

Nic nodded. 'But he does have a great car, a ter-rific sidekick and a cat-woman. Maybe I am The

Batman, but I'll have to decide which one of you is a robin and which is a cat.'

They went up the lift, which opened into the kitchen. Doc pushed a button on a remote control, and the glass doors recessed into the walls, providing a 180° view of the city of Adelaide below.

Nic, Rose and Sandy stepped into the open air. 'Nice place you have here, Doc.'

'Thanks, Nic, It's too big for me these days since I lost my best friend, Colin. We were together for forty-five years, married for forty. It's about time I sold up and moved somewhere a little smaller.'

Rose piped up. 'Like Government House?'

'Nope, but that's funny, Rose. I was thinking more like Mt Lofty House, but it would be too cold in them thar hills. Let's get to my library, and I'll run through the bird stuff with you.'

Rose grinned. 'Can we see your live birds first? I haven't seen a singing budgie up close, well, not since we had front-row seats at the Kylie Minogue concert.'

'Gee, you're quite funny, Rose, or are you nervous about something?'

Sandy responded instead. 'She is Doc. In a couple of days, we're getting in your little RFDS plane, and I assume it doesn't have a parachute in the tail. Rose is not a good flyer.'

'That's not true. I'm a good flyer. I don't like the take-off and landings.'

'You don't have to worry. I'm a Doctor and can administer propofol.'

'Would you do that?'

'No, that stuff killed Michael Jackson. I'll just bore you to sleep with stories about my beautiful grandchildren.'

They followed the Doctor from the front deck toward a large aviary. A pair of cockatoos were in one section, and four budgerigars were in the other. The budgies were sitting in ceramic bowls along the back wall. 'These are my other children. There's Liesel, Louisa, Brigitta and Marta. The two cockies are Maria and Georg.'

Sandy laughed, and Rose realised whom they were referring to. 'I know those names. It's the show from the seventies. Um...the lead singer guy died recently. Was it The Partridge Family?'

This time Nic laughed. 'Not quite, you're talking about David Cassidy. Now, he was a good-looking rooster. The names of the birds were from the Von Trapp Family and the film 'The Sound of Music." Nic broke into the song 'The Hills Are Alive with the Sound of Music' and started twirling around the yard.

Doc shook her head. 'Stop that Nic. Besides, you're twirling in the wrong direction. OK, let's get down to business. If we were in America, these little birds would be called parakeets. The scientific name is Melopsittacus Undulatus from the Psittaculidae Family, and that ends your lesson for today. If you want to know more, google it.'

Nic grinned. 'OK, Doc, so it's more about the bird watching being a life experience rather than a life lesson.'

The Doc nodded. 'You've got that right, Mr Handsome. We aren't a Bird club that wants to learn stuff as most of us already know how things work.'

Rose looked at her. 'So if that's all we need to know, why did you bring us all this way?'

'Hey, your Mr Handsome told me on the plane that he'd recently sold a house in Brisbane. I thought he might like to see mine in case he was interested in having a nice place to stay.'

Nic smiled. 'Thanks for the offer, and maybe we can do it another time. At the moment, I've got my unit here in Adelaide.'

Rose shook her head, 'And your place in Brisbane and a place in Melbourne. Did you forget about those too?'

'Yep, I'm nearly forty, you know.'

Doc looked at him, 'I thought you were much older, just from all those worry lines on your face.'

Nic looked at her. 'You should have seen my face before I met these two, it was as smooth as that Johnny Walker Red we were almost drinking.'

Rose interjected. 'Enough you two. What else will we have to do before flying up to Broken Hill?'

Nic grinned. 'Well, we could go to McLaren Vale or the Barossa Valley and try some wineries, or we could just spend more time studying the birds. We're supposed to be twitchers, so we should at least know what we are looking at and looking for.'

Doc shook her head. 'That doesn't sound like fun, but you do what you must do. Do you need access to a car?'

'Thanks, but I can get hold of one from a Rental Company.'

'Nope, take one of mine. I've got a couple of others in the basement. You can have your choice, Mr Handsome. There's a little pink one that you might like.'

They returned to the basement, Doc pressed a button on the wall, and another door slid open revealing four more cars: A late model Daimler, a 1970 Rolls Royce Silver Shadow, a 1966 Mercedes 230SL and an E-Type Jaguar convertible, but none were pink.

Doc took a step back. 'I now recognise you guys. You were at the Adelaide Motor Show selling those American Ex-Army Hummers last year. I thought I'd seen the three of you before.'

Nic looked at her. 'Oops.'

'OK, I'm only kidding about the pink one. Take whichever you want, except for the DeLorean, the Mercedes, and the Lotus, as they only have two seats. The Jag, Rolls and Daimler are too large on the skinny Adelaide CBD streets, but you are welcome to take my son's car. It's the pink Volkswagen Beetle.'

Sandy looked at her. 'You mean the QANTAS Pilot we met flying to Perth drives a little pink Beetle?'

'Well, it's a present for my granddaughter, but she's only ten and doesn't drive yet. You can return it to me on Monday when we fly to Broken Hill. Just park it at the airport. I'll meet you there.'

Nic nodded. 'Yep, the little pink bug will suit us fine. Thanks, Doc.'

They located the car, drove it from the basement, waved to the Doc and headed back to the city. Rose was sitting on the passenger side. 'So what are we going to do now?'

Nic grinned. 'Well, it's a beautiful day. We're driving in a beautiful car, and I've just spent a great afternoon with a couple of beautiful birds.'

Sandy called out from the rear seat. 'We've spent time with us before. Have you forgotten already? Your age is really taking its toll.'

Nic shook his head. 'No, I meant the two cockatoos, Georg and Maria.'

hey spent the next two days at the State Library looking and learning about bird watching and bird smuggling.

Nic had insisted that they took a break every hour to maintain their focus, and he did test them at the end. They all failed, including Nic, and he had set the questions.

It was now early Sunday afternoon, and Sandy finally had enough. 'I didn't expect this to be so depressing. It's terrible that the smugglers try to get past security. I've just encountered a couple that wrapped the birds in plastic sleeves and stuck them to their legs with sticky tape. They looked like two cowboys trying to shuffle their way through customs. The birds, on the other hand, are magnificent. It's such a shame we're seeing the ugly side of it.'

Rose nodded. 'My worst one was the plastic Coca-Cola bottles. One group had stuffed two galahs in one two-litre container and got caught with at least twenty birds.'

Sandy stood up and stretched. 'It's after three, so Rose and I are off to get changed for dinner. Would you like to come and meet my father? We're having dinner with him tonight.'

Nic nodded. 'Sure, and I promise to be on my best behaviour. Where are you going?'

Sandy smiled. 'Louca's in Pultney Street.'

Nic nodded. 'Good choice. I'll meet you guys there at seven.'

CHAPTER 20

Rose and Sandy had decided they needed new outfits for dinner and took an Uber to the Scanlan Theodore Boutique at the Burnside Village Shopping Centre. Sandy purchased a navy Blue Crepe Knit dress, and Rose decided on a dark green Tinsel Boucle outfit. They kept the receipts in case Nic needed them.

They arrived at the restaurant just before seven, and the host showed them their seats. They were in a private room, and Nic was already there, dressed in Armani.

Sandy saw her father arrive at the reception desk a few minutes later, but he didn't make eye contact, so she approached him and they walked back to their table.

'Nic, this is my Father and my favourite superhero, Robb Fraser.'

The men acknowledged each other, and then Nic and Robb sat down. 'So, Nic, tell me about yourself and how you manage to take these two around Australia without getting them into too much trouble.'

'I certainly will, Robb, but first, please let's order a drink. Name your poison.'

'I'll start with a whisky, neat. Glen Fiddich Reserve, please.'

Nic called over the maître d'. 'I saw Sullivan's Cove Whisky was on your list. Can we have two, neat, and a bottle of sparkling wine, please?'

The waiter walked away, and Robb looked at Nic. 'You just ignored my suggestion, son. I'm not sure about that.'

Sandy took a deep breath. 'That I did, and I know that Glen Fiddich is premium, but tonight, I want to thank you for allowing me to be a part of Sandy and Rose's life. This whisky is Tasmanian, and I thought you might like to try Australian instead.'

Sandy looked at the wine list and it was $65 per glass. 'Sip it slowly, Dad.' Her father laughed.

Nic took a breath. 'OK, Robb, I have been doing what I do for over ten years. I have never lost anyone and never intend to, although occasionally, they get a little wet or bloodied. I make sure it is all under my control at all times.'

'Good to know, but tell me more about the man, not the game.'

Nic looked over to Rose and Sandy, then back at Mr Fraser. 'I used to work for the Australian Security Intelligence Organisation.'

Sandy gasped, and Rose added. 'So, you are an ex-ASIO spy, Mr Nice Guy?'

'Not quite Rose. I was a spy in Afghanistan, but not anymore. I've mentioned before that I came back early from only a six-month stint after a couple of baddies had played tic-tac-toe on my knees and elbows, and there's a little more to that story. I wasn't supposed to get caught, and the people I worked for didn't like it, so they immediately brought me home.'

Robb took a long sip of his whisky. 'Well, then, Nic, Sandy tells me there is a lot more to your story. Do you answer to someone else? Someone higher up the food chain?'

'Not quite. I don't report to any one person directly. Sometimes I have to make reports, but I try to avoid paperwork. In my line of work, you learn not to leave evidence.' Nic let out a breath. 'Wow, that's more than I've told anyone about my history in a long time.'

Robb leaned forward. 'So, have you killed people? That makes a big difference to me.' Nic didn't respond as the waiter came up to take their orders. The table went quiet.

Nic shook his head slowly and he responded to the last question once the waiter moved away. 'I'm sorry, Robb, I will not answer that last question.'

'What question will you answer? Will Sandy and Rose ever be in danger?'

Nic nodded. 'That's another good question. I can only guarantee they will always be safe, even after this ends.'

Robb smiled and then Sandy stood up, walked over to her father, and hugged him around the shoulders.

Rose leaned over and gave Nic a quick peck on his cheek. He looked at her. 'What was that for?'

'I think you needed it.'

Sandy sat back down again, called the waiter over, and he brought over four glasses of Moet, and Sandy raised her champagne flute.

'To Nic and Robb, the two men in our lives.'

They chatted about Sandy's upbringing and made fun of Rose's disastrous three-day marriage as a nineteen-year-old. Nothing more was said about Nic's background, but as they waited for the bill to be settled, Nic noticed Sandy had taken a deep breath.

'You didn't ask about what happened to me here in Adelaide or why my ex-partner is serving nineteen years in Yatala Labour Prison.' Nic noticed that Robb was about to intervene. 'No, Robb, I don't need to know.'

They thanked the staff for their service and went outside. Nic made a phone call, and a white Holden Statesman met them at the kerb within a few minutes.

'Your ride sir. If you need anything, give me a call. The driver will take you home.' Robb looked at him. 'How do you know where I live?'

Rose interrupted. 'Nic knows stuff, does stuff, and gets stuff done. Finding out where you live would be easy for him.'

'Actually, I have to confess something, when Sandy sent you the link with Rose pirouetting through the waterfall in Brisbane, a location worm was attached, and everyone who has opened it since has had their details retained, so we know where they are. I can get someone to remove it remotely if you like.'

Robb shook his head. 'That's fine, leave it.' Then he stepped into the car and looked up at them. 'Just remember, with great power comes great responsibility, and that's a quote directly from Spiderman.'

Nic laughed, and they watched the car drive away, then another Holden Statesman came to the kerb, and he nodded towards it. 'This one's your chariot.'

Rose and Sandy stepped into the car, and the driver looked up. 'Where to? The Casino or to Rosey's nightclub in Hindley Street?'

Nic leaned forward. 'Neither. Please take them around the corner to Majestic Hotel, then you can drop me off in Angas Street.'

Rose smiled. 'So, where are you off to? Are you catching up with Commissioner Gordon and Batman? It is almost ten o'clock, you know.'

'No, but I think you mean Police Commissioner Steldons?'

Rose grinned. 'Sorry, and I assume he's now retired from his Batman duties. Does he still use the red iPhone?'

The Uber driver looked at them, wondering what they were talking about, but said nothing.

Rose and Sandy were dropped at their Hotel, and Nic was delivered to the Police Headquarters in Angas Street.

The Duty Sergeant let him in and led him through to the office of The Commissioner. Nic knocked and entered.

'Good to see you again, Nic. Please take a seat. I heard about the wine scamming thing you just wound up in Perth and that reptile smuggling, too. You've been busy since you were last here. What has brought you back to Adelaide?'

Nic shook his hand. 'Bird smuggling, Gerry. We're flying off to Broken Hill, then driving over to Boolcoomatta Reserve, but that's not why I'm here. I'd need a favour and would like to look something up on the Police Database.'

The Commissioner nodded. 'Is it something or someone?'

'Well, it's something Sandy was involved in years ago. She told me her ex was still in Yatala Prison for a long stretch. My computer guy could find out for me, but I'd prefer it was my eyes only.'

'I assume you still have your ASIO Security Clearance?' Nic nodded. 'Yes.'

The Commissioner logged on, Nic keyed in his access number, and then they located Sandy's details. The database brought up a reference to a Court Case from 2014 that included the sentencing details of the perpetrator. They reviewed the reports. 'He's one nasty dude.'

'I've got enough info, thanks, Gerry. Why are you here so late?'

The Commissioner nodded. 'I'm always first in and last to leave. My men and women deserve it, and thanks for the red iPhone as it keeps things a little less dark. It's still surprising that after all these years, everyone still remembers the Police Commissioner in that campy '60s Batman series.'

The Duty Sergeant led Nic back outside, and as he walked back to his apartment he wondered if he could keep everything under control.

andy parked the pink Beetle and left the keys with the Airport Valet service, then they made their way to the Royal Flying Doctor Service terminal.

Doc was waiting for them. 'I'm glad you came, it's just over an hour to fly the five hundred kilometres, so we'll arrive just before lunch. FYI, there are no patients on the flight.'

Sandy looked at her. 'What, no drinks service on board? But seriously, how come there aren't any patients?'

'It's a relocation flight. It's just been here in Adelaide for a service. You'll keep me company, and if Nic takes control, it goes towards his flying hours.'

Rose looked at her. 'He can't fly. He was drinking last night.'

Nic nodded. 'Yep, good call Rose. I broke into the apartment next door and skulled the contents in the bar fridge. They only had cheap whiskey, though.'

'That's your sister's place, Nic.'

'I know right? What a waste of time that was.'

Doc nodded. 'Good to know. So, are you guys ready?'

Doc noted their lack of luggage. 'Where's your sleeping kit?'

Rose pointed over to the carry-on suitcases. 'We've packed light. Nic didn't say anything about having to stay out in the open, and we shouldn't be there very long.'

Doc grinned. 'We're not in a tent, Rose. I've got a Winnebago waiting for us in Broken Hill. It sleeps eight, and there are only four of us, but we'll pick up a couple of stragglers. Don't worry, they're good fun.'

CHAPTER 21

They made their way down the plane. Doc went through the pre-flight checks in the cockpit, and Nic sat beside her. They donned the headphones, and she taxied the aircraft to the runway.

This is VH- HDD. Seeking clearance take off.

Doc turned around to Sandy and Rose and saw they were holding hands. She smiled. 'We'll touch down in about an hour, Rose, but you might enjoy it more if you open your eyes.'

'I'm good, Doc. Just take it easy when we take off, please.'

'We're already airborne.'

Just over an hour later, Doc started the descent into Broken Hill. She pointed out the Bird Sanctuary down below, and they then flew over the border crossing.

Nic turned around to them. 'You'll have to put your watches onto New South Wales time Rose, and your phones too. Watch your phones to see when they change over.'

Rose stared at her phone, and Sandy realised what was going on. 'Thanks, Nic.'

Doc laughed. 'Don't believe everything Mr Handsome says.'

Rose muttered through clenched teeth. 'We have to believe it. Even the stuff he makes up.'

Doc brought the plane down to a soft landing, and there was a welcoming party waiting for them. 'OK, Mr Handsome, you're about to meet the rest of my gang, but be careful with the tall one as she's looking for her next husband. She likes them tall, dark and handsome, but don't worry, I'm the youngest at sixty-eight.'

Nic looked at the three women coming towards him. They were all tall. 'Thanks for the heads up, but I think I'll have to play that Rose is my new partner, Sandy is my sister, and we're all twitchers on our honeymoon.'

Sandy looked at him. 'That won't quite work. I'm blond, so how can you be my brother?'

'I dye my hair.'

Sandy nodded. 'Given you're nearly forty and all. 'Just for Men' will remove the grey and wash that man right out of your hair.'

Doc shook her head. 'You guys are a scream. Look out, Nic, here come the girls.'

The tallest of the women ignored Sandy, Rose and even Doc, and went straight up to Nic, hugging him. 'Hello, Mr Handsome. The Doc has already told me all about you. She told me you're not married either.'

Nic looked over to Rose. 'Looks like I just got divorced, Rose. Sorry about that.' Rose shrugged.

'OK then, Mr Handsome. Who are these two young ones? Your sisters?'

Nic laughed. 'Nup, they're my closest friends, Sandy and Rose. Please don't be upset. They forced me to bring them along. We're all new to this twitching stuff.'

The other two women came up to Nic and surrounded him. 'Hey Doc, we've got one of those...um... what do you call them? You know, that haven't experienced the wicked ways of our wacky world?'

Doc laughed. 'Our next husbands?'

Rose and Sandy collected their luggage and watched the four women usher Nic towards the airport building. He had left his luggage behind, then stopped and turned around. 'Are you two coming? And please bring the luggage.'

Rose and Sandy collected his luggage and caught up with them. They went to where the Motorhome was parked. It was a behemoth.

Nic climbed up the steps and called Rose and Sandy to step inside. Doc called out. 'There's a double bed at both ends and three single beds on the sides.'

A scruffy little dog went past them, clambered down the steps, and jumped into one of the women's arms.

Doc then stepped inside with them. 'Yes, and the sides come back in as well. It makes it easier to drive. Would you like to drive it, Mr Handsome?' Nic shrugged.

The group stepped back outside and approached the front of the vehicle. Doc pointed up to the name written across the front of the car. It read '*The Tin Man.*'

'That was my idea, Mr Handsome,' one of the women whispered to Nic. 'I'm Dorothy, and this little brindle Terrier is Toto.' She put the dog back down on the ground. 'The other two ladies are Katherine with a K and Wendy with a Woo.'

All seven were now in the Motorhome, and Doc looked at Nic. 'Before we work out the sleeping arrangements, who's up for a cuppa?'

Nic nodded. 'Make mine Chai Tea, thanks Doc.'

'Nope, too early for that, Mr Handsome. I'm talking about the good stuff.'

Doc opened one of the overhead cupboards and brought down a bottle of Johnny Walker Red, then collected eight glasses and poured a dram in each. They each collected their drinks and raised them for the toast.

Wendy spoke first. 'To men, life, lovers, and never the twain shall meet.'

Nic smiled, then raised his glass. 'To women and the enigmas that you all are.'

Rose looked at the eighth glass. 'Who is that for?

Doc sighed. 'To a long life and our good health. That's why we always pour it in case this is our last drink.'

Rose then went down to the rear of the Motorhome and back again. 'This is bigger than my first apartment out of Uni. I was living with two other people, so we took turns breathing in and out.'

Doc laughed, 'You crack me up, Rose. Why have you not leapt into the fairy tale they call marriage?' Rose sighed. 'I was married once, Doc. It lasted three days, and I still haven't forgiven my parents for making me do it. My dear old father needed to win a business deal.'

Doc nodded. 'What about you Sandy?'

'I don't want to talk about it if that's OK.'

Nic moved over to her and put his arm around her waist. 'Enough of this sad stuff, Sandy. I've got bigger worries. Like where am I going to sleep without being in the way?'

Dorothy pointed towards the two driver seats. 'They fold down to make a single bed. I don't think it would be a good idea if we had you in a double by yourself.' Nic nodded. 'Good choice.'

Dorothy continued. 'Sandy and Rose can share one double, and I'll take the other one. Doc and Katherine use the singles as they've done it before. Oh, and by the way, Nic, there's only one toilet in here, so you'll have to use the ablution tent on site or do the other thing that men do where they are in the bush.'

'What's that? Whistle loudly?'

'Yes, let's call it that.'

Rose piped up. 'Nic doesn't like sharing bathrooms, Dorothy.'

'Well, he'll have the whole Sanctuary if he needs it. Jump in the driver's seat, Mr Handsome and I'll teach you how to drive a bus full of crazy women.'

They took their seats around the RV and then the four women started singing, '*The wheels on the bus go round and round.*' Nic turned the key and started the behemoth. 'It's pretty quiet, Dorothy. Are you sure it's on?'

Dorothy nodded. 'I had it converted over to electric earlier this year. A dozen or so solar panels are on the roof, and it hardly costs anything to run. Head for Highway A32, Mr Handsome, then turn toward Dome Rock.'

Wendy looked at Rose and Sandy. 'You guys don't seem the twitching type. I get Mr Handsome, as he might get sick of being stared at by all the city folk, but Rose and Sandy, you two don't seem the outdoorsy types.' They didn't comment.

A little later Nic turned off the highway and pulled into a resting area. 'I have had enough of driving this tin whale and I need to tell you guys why we are here.'

Dorothy nodded. 'OK, Mr Handsome, we'll take a wee break. You might find a tree if need to, and by the time you come back, we'll have boiled the kettle and set up for lunch.'

Nic stepped down from the driver's side, and Rose and Sandy moved outside with him. 'I think we'll have to bring them in with us guys. The budgie smuggling is bigger than what we can handle. If it's an inside job, I don't think these four would be a part of it.'

Rose nodded. 'We've only been in the RV for less than half an hour.'

'Yep, but I can't see why the women would wear budgie smugglers.'

The others had set up a table, put on a table-cloth, spread some lunch and unfolded eight chairs. 'Lunch is up. Come and get it.'

Nic took a sandwich and remained standing and the others waited for him to speak. 'OK, guys. Rose, Sandy and I are here on behalf of the Australian Budgerigar Society and the Australian Border Police. There is some chatter that a budgie smuggling operation is being run from here, so we've been brought in to have a look and shut it down.'

Doc added. 'I've seen what these guys do. I was just over in Margaret River, and they brought down a wine scammer that had been in operation for over two years. Mr Hansome and his associates took them down in three days.'

'Thanks, Doc, but this one may be a little harder as we have no idea if it will happen whilst we are here, and it could just be a waste of time.'

Dorothy responded. 'There's no such thing as wasted time at our age, Mr Handsome. We've all recently lost our partners and are living every day as it comes.'

They all nodded including Rose and Sandy, so Nic continued. 'Has something or someone come to your attention lately? It could be someone new to the club. Have any of you got access to the member registrations?'

Dorothy nodded. 'We all have. It's all on the website, but you can't get access to it out here.'

Nic smiled. 'I've got a guy in Melbourne that will if you are OK with it.'

Doc interrupted. 'Won't you need a password or something? How will you get in touch with him?'

'Nup, he will get in without it and won't leave a trace. I have a Satellite phone, so he should be able to contact me. Is there a list of attendees for this week's event?'

Doc smiled. 'Yes, but it's pretty flexible. We don't expect people to turn up if they find something else to do. It's just a destination rather than a commitment.'

Nic nodded. 'Are there any photographs from the last campsite showing the new members?'

'Yes, on my iPad. We take a photo at the start, then at the end, so we know who had stayed for the whole time. Do you want to look at them now?'

'Yes, please.'

Doc opened up her photo folder and went through to the last camp. It was date-stamped about three months ago. Nic located the pictures taken on the first day and the previous day, then changed the images so they were side by side. so the same people were accounted for. They went through them, looking for any anomalies.

'OK, Doc. Which of these guys are new to the club?'

Doc pointed them out as there were only five, from the twenty-three.

'Do you know their names yet?'

'Nope, but their details will be on the database. I can work it out from there.'

Katherine came up. 'Those two standing on the left were the couple from Orange, Mavis and John something? I remember they were driving in a car that was too small for the size of their caravan. The other three I can't remember exactly but two were a couple, and the last was by himself.'

Rose was now leaning into having a look as well. 'Hey Nic, one thing, you can't see their faces in both photos as they're not in the same spot. The guy on the left tries to hide his face behind the woman in front of the first one, and his head is down in the second photo. The woman has a cap on in both shots, but you can't see her face. That single guy is sitting at the front in the second picture, but we can't see his face either.'

Doc nodded. 'Well spotted Rose. You're certainly good at this stuff.'

'Thanks, Doc, I've just learned to look better. Sandy and I used to have a clothing boutique store in Brisbane. It was called 'The She Shed'. We were better at that rather than this budgie smuggling and scam investigation stuff.'

Wendy and Katherine laughed. 'Is that what you all came for? Just to look into budgie smugglers? We've both spent time at Sydney beaches and so did the ex-Prime Minister, Tony Abbott. We've seen it all before.'

Nic nodded. 'Rose and Sandy showed me the pictures again. I'm scarred for life.'

Doc grinned. 'Come on, Mr Handsome, man up. You must have seen worse in your work, and besides it's your turn to do the dishes. We've even got an apron for you if you want one.'

Doc then handed him an apron with 'Kiss the Cook' on it, tied the bow at the back and gave him a peck on the cheek. 'Thanks, Doc.'

Nic looked towards the others who had also lined up behind her. All of them were smiling and waiting their turn, including Rose and Sandy. Sandy then looked at the eighth chair. 'I assume it's out just in case it's the last time you sit down?'

'Yes, it is.' This time, it came from Wendy.

Sandy and Rose helped Nic pack up the lunch dishes, and they climbed back into the motorhome. Nic was in the back with Sandy and Rose, Dorothy was driving, and Toto was sitting in a dog harness in the passenger seat. They were at the turnoff to Boolcoomatta Reserve in less than half an hour.

'Almost there, guys, so you can stop asking if we're there yet.'

They drove on a dirt road heading towards the campsite, passed the sign to Dome Rock and the motorhome bottomed out. Dorothy looked back. 'Oops. It must be the extra baggage, or it might just be that it's the first time in a long time that a fine man is in here with us. This old girl might be complaining a bit.'

Nic asked, 'Are you talking about yourself or the bus?'

'It could have been Tin Man or you, Mr Handsome. You choose.'

Dorothy found a site large enough to accommodate the motorhome and pulled to a stop. 'We're in the middle of nowhere, but at least someone knew we were coming. They've set up the toilet tent just for Nic.'

She turned off the engine, undid Toto's harness, and let him out the door. The rest of the crew climbed out, and Sandy watched as Toto did a few circles, then moved under the motorhome and sat down in the shade under the vehicle.

'Smart dog that one. He knows how to keep cool.'

'Yes, and he also knows we are in a National Park where dogs aren't allowed. So you won't see him around much. He'll be invisible.'

Rose looked at Nic. 'We worked with someone in Adelaide who kept himself invisible, maybe they went to the same superhero school?'

'Not likely, Toto went to school in Mt Gambier, and we ain't in Kansas anymore.'

'Good to know Dorothy.'

Nic looked at Rose. 'That's from the Wizard of Oz, Rose. You know 'Follow the Yellow Brick Road.'

Rose gave a wry smile. 'But we're on a dirt track, so there's no yellow or bitumen road around here. God, if you only had a brain.'

This brought laughter out of all the women, and Toto gave a little woof. 'What did I say?'

Dorothy responded. 'Haven't you seen the film, Rose? So you don't get the connection between me, Toto, and my motorhome being called 'The Tin Man?''

Rose shrugged. 'I wasn't allowed to watch much television as a kid.'

Dorothy looked at her. 'The film was released in 1939.'

'Wow, that's way before my time.'

Nic smiled, then looked around at the other caravans and motorhomes in the area. 'Have you seen the van that the couple from the photo are in?'

Dorothy shook her head. 'Not me, Mr Handsome, but they don't have to stay with the rest of the group. They could be at least three hundred metres away as we have to set a limit for safety and privacy.'

'OK, maybe later we go for a moonlight stroll around the campsite. Any takers?'

'I'll go Mr Handsome.'

'Me too.'

'Me, three.'

'Me, four.'

Sandy and Rose said nothing, and in the meantime, other twitchers had moved towards the group. Doc pointed out the President. 'The young guy with the field glasses around his neck is Goose. We call him that because he tends to honk the horn on his Jeep too much when he gets stuck in the convoy of caravans.'

Dorothy looked at Nic. 'He'll know about the couple hiding in the photos.'

'Maybe, but don't ask him about it. We don't know anything about anything until we need to know something. Leave it to me, please.'

Dorothy nodded and Rose looked at her. 'Did you understand that, Dorothy?'

oose came up and introduced himself to Nic, Rose and Sandy. 'They call me Goose because I'm unflappable.' Nic heard Doc stifle a cough. 'So Goose, is everyone here yet? When do we go looking for the budgies?'

'Well, it's the same group of twenty-three from last time. Twenty-six, now that you guys are here.'

Nic nodded. 'We saw a couple of new members in a photo and thought we may have met them at another Bird Sanctuary. Do you know them?'

'Not yet, as they mainly stay by themselves and are always first to arrive and last to leave. They must be cold in their old Bedford Van, though.

They didn't make those old buses with air-conditioning or heaters. They're a bit odd too. They told me they were husband and wife, but they looked more like brother and sister, but they could be from Tasmania.' He laughed at his comment.

Doc felt the conversation may be getting away from Nic, so she took over. 'So what are their names again, Goose?'

Goose continued. 'I think the guy is Griff, and the woman is Kerry. Oh, and the other guy that keeps to himself, his name is Dally or something like that.'

CHAPTER 22

Rose realised they'd had dealings with a trio of the same names in Tasmania. It was the scam that had introduced them to BB Kingsman. The man named Griff had been buying up land to build a resort in the pristine wilderness. He was also painting the hindquarters of dogs, spreading a rumour about a sighting of the extinct Tasmanian Tiger, and the locals were not happy about it.

Rose leaned toward Nic and whispered. 'Dallas was the bus driver from Burnie. Griff and Kerry are here, too? Surely it's not them?'

Nic shook his head subtly at Rose. 'Thanks, Goose, I don't know them, but hopefully, they'll be around when we light the bonfire tonight.'

'Nope, they never come to them. The Dally guy sometimes joins in but he stays in the background. He also turns up at dinner time, and mooches a meal wherever he can find it.'

Goose then moved away to catch up with some of the other crowd. Doc leaned into Nic. 'So Mr Handsome, do you want to take a walk? Maybe we can meet some other happy campers. Can I pass you off as my new boyfriend? It will give everyone a laugh.'

'Nup, sorry, Doc, on both counts. I've got to work out how to send the photos to my computer guy. He has a facial recognition programme that will confirm something for me about those new-comers.'

Dorothy piped up this time. 'You can get a signal from the top of Dome Rock, it's the highest point around here. There's a satellite that goes over every six hours. We found that out last time we were here. A group of us head up there before breakfast, watch the sunrise, google the crap out of our I-pads to catch up on the news, and send mes-sages back home. It's about an hour and a half re-turn hike from here.'

Nic nodded. 'Thanks, so when is the next satel-lite due?'

'About eleven p.m. tonight. I can show you the way if you like.' Rose stifled a laugh and waited for Nic's response. 'That's OK. I'll leave it until the morning then, and I assume we've got to look at the budgies first, don't we?'

'Probably, but they'll be here tomorrow, and maybe you won't be Mr Handsome, so let's go for that walk before we eat. Sandy and Rose can pre-pare the dinner.'

Sandy and Rose were about to object, but it was already too late as Dorothy and Doc had each en-twined one of Nic's arms, and Wendy and Kather-ine joined the line. They were singing '*We're off to see the Wizard*', and Toto trotted along behind.

Sandy looked at Rose. 'Do you think they'll bring him back?'

'I would say so. There's nothing out there but scrub, and Nic forgot to take his Satellite phone with him. I saw it in the motorhome on the kitchen bench, but that's the least of our worries. What are we going to prepare for dinner?'

They went back inside the motorhome and looked through the cupboards for inspiration. Rose opened the fridge and then shut it quickly. 'It looks like one of these ladies is a major Tupperware lover, Sandy.'

Rose opened the door again, then realised the door on the left was a freezer. 'And there's more in here.'

Sandy nodded, 'It looks like all we need to work out is how to operate the Microwave and defrost something. Everything has been labelled. Don't you love organised people?'

'Hey, I'm organised. I organised Nic to get us a Credit Card to spend his money.'

'True, but there's no ATM out this way to get the cash-out.'

Rose nodded. 'Damn the banks.'

They decided on vegetable lasagne and spanakopita, defrosted the dinners, set up the dining table outside and gathered eight chairs.

'Eight settings, Sandy, just in case it's their last meal and I believe The Batman is due to have dinner with us. I just saw the bat signal in the sky.'

'That was a real bat Rose. They're prolific out here.'

Rose stepped outside and started calling out. 'Batman, Batman, where for art thou?' Sandy tried to quieten her down. 'Sshh Rose, not everyone knows that the current South Australian Commissioner of Police is Batman doing a day job.'

They were sitting at the outside dining table, still waiting for the others to come back from their walk, so they brought out Nic's satellite phone to see if they could guess the password. Sandy was trying all the different combinations. '*R0se&N1c*', '*Sand1& N1c*', and then she looked at Rose. 'How about we try Nic's date of birth? Do you know it yet?'

'No, but he said he's thirty-six, so he must have been born in '84, but that's about it. I would say he's a Gemini. You know, he's good at everything he does and has lots of sex appeal.'

Sandy laughed. 'No, I would guess a Leo. Attention seeking, a natural leader and popular with all the ladies.'

They went back inside the motorhome to see if they could find the latest women's magazine for the most current horoscopes and to open the wine. They couldn't decide on red or white, so they opened a bottle of both.

Upon stepping back outside, Sandy noticed that Nic's satellite phone was no longer on the outside table.

'Did you pick up Nic's phone, Rose?'

'Nope. Why?'

'It's gone. It was at the head of the table.'

They started searching all around, then heard Nic and the ladies coming towards them, and they were singing loudly. *'Somewhere over the rainbow.'*

Nic bounded up to Rose and Sandy, gave them both a quick peck on their cheeks and whispered. 'What a hoot guys. All they want to do is sing, laugh and tell really bad dad jokes. Did anything happen whilst I was away with the lady munchkins?'

Rose stated quickly, 'We've lost your Sat phone.'

'It's on the kitchen table. I left it there on the charger.'

'Yes, but we had it out here trying to guess the password.'

'Did you get it open?'

Rose shook her head. 'Nope, but you're more worried about us getting into the phone rather than it's been stolen?'

'It's got a tracker in it, so unless a kleptomaniac kangaroo picked it up and stuffed it in her pouch, it will turn up somewhere.'

Sandy hugged him. 'Can I buy you a new one if it doesn't? What do they cost?'

'Don't worry about it. I'll get Chewy to run the locator on it.'

'But you can't ring him, you dope.'

y now, the ladies were sitting around the table and enjoying wine served by Sandy and Rose. Doc had overheard the dilemma about the phone.

'Hey Mr Handsome, 'The Tin Man' has a CB Radio, so you can get onto your computer guy that way. Otherwise, we can wait until eleven p.m. and walk to Blueberry Hill and ring from there.'

Rose shook her head. 'I don't think Nic's looking for his thrill on Blueberry Hill tonight, Doc.'

The group looked at her, but Dorothy called out first. 'Rose, you just made another musical reference. We could use you at the quiz night at the local.'

'Thanks, Dorothy, but I stopped listening to music the day the music died.'

'Wow, drop the mike. Another one, is American Pie, by Don McLean. Great song.'

Nic nodded. 'Stop it, Rose, you're just showing off now. Can I use the CB Radio, please, Dorothy?'

Dorothy nodded. 'Sure, but we're all set on a common channel, so all and sundry will hear your secret chatter.'

'It's all good. I can use Morse code and get things underway.' Nic left the group, went inside and started clicking on the microphone.

After a couple of minutes, he had a response and Rose had been watching. 'How did you do that? Chewy wouldn't be expecting a message in Morse code from a CB radio.'

'Nope, but he knows that we're here, so I kept hopping across the country until I found someone that knew Chewy's call code, then they rang him.'

'Does he know we're in trouble? Do you have a secret squirrel call code?'

'Yep. It's Chewbacca - please save Anakin again.''

'I've no idea what that means, Nic, but I'm glad you've got in contact.'

The clicking started again, and Nic was writing down the letters. He stopped, then looked at Rose and nodded. 'Well, the phone is here somewhere, which is good.'

'Why?'

'It means my kleptomaniac kangaroo theory is busted. It would have hopped well out of range by now.'

They went back outside and finished dinner.

he group then stood up, grabbed a couple more bottles of red wine, and headed towards the camp bonfire.

Rose looked at Nic. 'I thought we were in a National Park. They shouldn't be lighting a fire.'

Nic nodded. 'They are only banned at certain times. Besides that, I've got the marshmallows and have warmed up my vocal cords and drinking arm.'

Rose hesitated. 'But what if Kerry, Griff or Dallas are there? They might know we're onto them.'

Nic shook his head. 'They won't be there if they are the budgie smugglers. They won't be anywhere near anyone.'

The seven joined the crowd around the fire, and Nic noticed that Doc had made a beeline towards

Goose. They had a few words, and Goose was now making his way over to him. 'So, Doc tells me that you are suspicious of new members being part of a budgie smuggling syndicate?'

'Not quite Goose. I'm just here to look at the birds.'

'OK, Mr Smart-guy, or whomever you think you are. This is my show, and these are my terms. You either fill us all into your little charade, or I get your little group into my truck and drive you back to Broken Hill.'

'Fair enough, Goose, but can you give me until the morning once everyone is a little more sober, and it's not so dark.'

Goose considered the options. 'Sure. The next satellite passes over at five in the morning. We'll meet up on top of Dome Rock and sort this out.' Nic nodded, looked at Rose and Sandy, and approached them. 'The show is over for tonight, guys, that's unless you want to hang around and do some singing?' Rose and Sandy couldn't get back to the motorhome quickly enough.

CHAPTER 23

Nic's watch alarm went off just after 4 a.m. and they dressed for the hike to Dome Rock. Dawn was breaking, and there was enough light for people to watch the sunrise. Several four-wheel drives were parked nearby, and fortunately, they had left the other ladies in the motor home wearing off last night's night.

Rose nodded to the waiting crowd. 'There are at least ten people up here, and that's a bit disappointing.'

Nic sighed. 'I was hoping Goose would keep it on the down low, but this would probably be the most exciting thing since there was a rumour that the white-browed treecreeper was in the local vicinity.'

'Is that real, Nic, or did you just make it up?'

'Rose, you must believe everything I tell you, not just the stuff I make up.'

Goose came up to them. 'One of the guys told me the Bedford van was on the move early this morning, as he'd heard it chugging away. They probably have a few hours on us, but they won't get far. They are heading northwest, and it's only a four-wheel drive track up that way. What do you want us to do?'

'Actually, I'd prefer it if you did nothing. We don't know what this is. They may have just decided to leave.'

'OK, there is that, but I had my suspicions. I mean, we're supposed to be a social club that watches birds, so why come all this way if you're not going to join in?'

Nic nodded. 'I think I know what you mean. How long before we get better light?'

'Another twenty minutes. Why, what are you thinking Mr Thorn? Freelance Investigator and former ASIO spy?'

Nic nodded. 'So, Doc told you?'

Goose said nothing. 'All right then, Goose, do you have a drone? We'll need to see how far they have got.'

A chorus of voices broke the silence. 'Yes, we do.'

One of the men stepped forward, then another, and Goose pulled a drone out of his backpack. 'Yes, Mr Thorn. Here's one we prepared earlier, and once it hits five a.m., the satellite should give us enough signal to find them.'

The two men went through their start-up routines, and soon, their little buzzing copters were airborne.

Goose hadn't started his up and directed Nic to move away from the others for a one-on-one. 'So, Mr Thorn, is this all something to do with the South Australian Parks and Wildlife using the spray on Micro-Dot Technology stuff about six months ago? The trial was part of my idea to keep track of the birds, not just the smuggled ones. Many breeders do like to know where their stock came from as it avoids in-breeding, that sort of stuff.'

'Yep. It's a great idea, and there are many other applications it can be used with.'

Goose smiled. 'Thanks. I helped them net the flock that they used for the sampling process. We coated a hundred birds for the trial. Have some of them been found in other places already?'

'Yep, that's what brought me here. A couple of budgies turned up in a pet shop in Asia, so my guys sent an officer over there to find out where they originated from. When she ran the scanner over the feathers, it was determined that the birds came from here. Of course, the shop trader had no idea how he obtained them and had no papers of the origin or the importation approval.'

'Interesting isn't it? Do you think they'd realise they would be caught? Do you reckon Griff, Kerry and Dally are part of it?'

'Well, it's looking more likely given they seem to be making a run for it, and hopefully, their Bedford van is not full of birds, but if it is, we can release them back into their same habitat.'

Goose nodded, returned to the other two men operating their drones, and started up his own. 'OK, we know they are heading northwest, so I'm sending my drone out that way. Dom, can you send yours straight up, and Wally, send yours due north.'

After a couple of minutes, Dom called out. 'I've got them. They're stuck in the old river track. It's a four-wheel drive only through there, so they must be desperate to escape. I reckon they're about two kilometres away.'

They brought back their drones and started towards their vehicles. Sandy, Rose and Nic climbed into Goose's Jeep, and the convoy headed off.

Nic flicked on the two-way. 'This is Ranger Smith on Channel 19. We're hunting for some brazen budgie boofheads and they have gone AWOL. Come back.'

There was no reply.

'Hey, Yogi Bear in the Bedford van. It looks like you're stuck with your hand in a pic-a-nic basket. Come back.'

Again, no reply.

He tried again. 'This is Nic Thorn, and on behalf of the South Australia Parks and Wildlife Service, we know where you're located, Griff and Kerry. Come back.'

They heard a crackle on the radio. 'So, Nic Thorn, you finally found us. I thought we'd left you in Tasmania.'

CHAPTER 24

About 30 minutes later, their convoy arrived at the riverbed. Kerry was sitting in the van, and Griff and Dallas were still trying to dig their way out of being bogged in the soft sand.

Nic leaned over and pressed the horn in the Jeep, and the group looked up. Nic then stepped out but told Rose and Sandy to stay seated.

Nic called out. 'It's over this time, Griff.'

'How did you find us this time, Thorn?'

'Ask Dallas, as he stole my Satellite phone. It's got a tracker in it.'

Griff looked over to his brother. 'You idiot. I told you it was a set-up.'

'But Griff, I heard those two women. They said that the South Australian Commissioner of Police was due here soon. I had to get it off them so they couldn't ring him. He could arrest us, you know.'

Dallas pulled the phone from his back pocket and threw it at Nic. Rose overheard the comment and laughed. 'Hey Sandy, I didn't know The Batman was also the Invisible Man. Double the superhero. What a guy.'

Goose then directed Danny to drive his 4WD truck into the riverbed, and they hooked up the tow rope to get the van out.

Griff suddenly stopped them, opened the van's back doors, and lifted the flat wooden tray. It revealed a hidden compartment with rows of plastic cylinders containing budgerigars. Nic walked up and took pictures with his phone. Kerry and Dallas were then led to one of the other vehicles and told to sit in the back.

They released all the birds and watched them fly away, then retrieved the Bedford van from the soft sand, and one of the other men drove it to the camp.

When they arrived back, the rest of the adventurers gathered around and cheered when Nic stepped from the Jeep. He received a kiss on the cheek from each of the ladies, all fourteen of them.

Goose approached Nic. 'Thanks for all this, Mr Thorn. You and your team are welcome to stay for the duration. I know Doc and the ladies would appreciate it.'

'I'd love to Goose, but Nic Thorn and Associates have another scam to bust, so we have to be on our way back to Brisbane. I've got a plane coming to pick us up in two hours. Could you run us to the airstrip at the next-door sheep station?'

Rose came up to him. 'Damn you, Nic, are we flying back to Adelaide in a little buzz box?'

'Yep, sorry about that, but this time, the plane does have a parachute in the tail.'

'OK, anything else we need to know?'

'Yep. How do you feel about Xmas in July?'

DEDICATION

Again, thanks for making this journey with us. (Maybe next time, Rose, a little less conversation and more action please.) (Ah, Nic, that's a line from an Elvis Presley song. Have you heard of him?)

Please keep reading for an excerpt from the next adventures of Nic Thorn & Associates in 'Five Mouldy Bins'

<u>Five Mouldy Bins</u>

It was mid-July, around noon, and another cloudless winter's day in Brisbane, South East Queensland. Rosemary Palmer was surrounded by happiness but it was too early for Christmas.

Rose was standing in a dark green cardboard box surrounded by Christmas decorations. The box was waist-high, full of baubles and Rose's arms were held out at ninety degrees with red and green tinsel dripping from them.

A small crowd of old timers were gathered around, taking turns throwing more tinsel over her head. One of the gentlemen shuffled forward with a big grin and a sprig of mistletoe in his hand.

Rose looked at him and wondered how she would get out of kissing him, after all, it was the tradition. 'Hello Mr Cook, how is your wife these days? Is she here somewhere? Is that why you have the mistletoe?'

The man stopped mid-stride, looked at his hand, then at Rose. 'This isn't mistletoe, young lady. It's my lunch. I'm a vegan you know.' He shuffled off, shaking his head, and began munching on the festive sprig.

An announcement then interrupted the Christmassy chaos: 'Welcome to The Hamilton Village Retirement Centre. It's Christmas in July, Ladies and Gentlemen, boys and girls. Santa will be arriving within the hour.'

A toddler was now standing in front of Rose, and she tried her best not to stare down at the boy, but eventually conceded to his cheeky charm. 'If you like I can give you some of this tinsel, and you can pretend you are a Christmas tree, too.'

The boy looked at her and squirmed a little. 'My dad told me not to talk to strangers, and you look very strange dressed as a tree, but the man there told me to ask you something.'

Rose looked over to her friend and business partner, Nic Thorn. He was dressed as an elf and gave her a silly grin. Rose looked back down at the boy. 'Sure, what is that little man?'

'How does Father Christmas get all the way around the world in one night?'

MORE READING

For more readings from the Nic Thorn & Associ-ates Investigations series:

One Tricked Phoney

Rose needed a +1, but not for the usual wed-ding/party. She was going to a funeral and needed a quiet, unassuming type. The best option was to use her dating site, but when Nic Thorn arrived, he was anything but a wallflower. These modern-day adventures lead them from one lively caper to another, involving portrait provenance, invoice in-accuracy, and a recycler's relapse, on their travels from Brisbane, Adelaide, to the SA border.

Two Hurtled Gloves

Nic has to investigate a wedded miss, the mis-guided pretence of Tiger tracking, and some bank-ing blasphemy. Rose was to be a bride again, but this time, Nic Thorn ensured it wasn't the short, fat and shallow man her parents forced her to marry the first time. Together with her BFF Sandy, they move onto another tale, tracking down the elusive and believed to be extinct Thylacine. Then Sandy loses her identity, and Nic introduces them to the benign world of banking.

Three French Bens

Nic's friend, Benoit Trudeau, is one-third of the 'Three French Bens'. He has just bought into a high-end restaurant, so he calls Nic's Team in to have a look, as the numbers look fishy, and they might have to go angling for the truth. Nic and his crew head to Rockhampton to help the Queensland Department of Agriculture look into some cattle duffing, as apparently, it's heard a lot up that way. Finally, Sandy has to deal with an old school friend or is that a fiend that has been taking a loan from her, at her expense?

Five Mouldy Bins

It's Christmas in July, and the Department of Health in Brisbane is concerned that someone may be stuffing their mattress with ill-gotten gains, so Nic and the team are brought in to bring it to a head – reindeer style. Sandy and Rose meet up with their 'friend' Dimond, who keeps handing over her hard-earned (well, she tells them that anyway) to lease a new rental property for her husband and family as it turns out, the Real Estate Agent knows how to manage to take the deposit too, but only ever in cash. Then, the team gets involved in a diamond scam.

Six Geezers Lying

Car insurance companies are driven up the wall by bogus claims and 'accidents' and it's about time someone gives the scammers a crash course on how to stop. One of the national restaurant chains puts together a competition so easy that anyone can win, then the team gets involved in an art scam, and Rose's Father is in the middle. Can he afford to have his reputation tarnished? Art is not always art, as it depends on your point of view, but fraud is always fraud.

Seven Hapless Hoops

Organisations keep looking to Nic Thorn and his Associates to sort stuff out. This time, one of his old friends calls upon him to locate his missing wife; but it is too close to home for Nic not to be in the right place to investigate. Meantime, a car vanishes without a trace, and a horse race is gathering pace, but will they be too late to save face?

AUTHORS BIOGRAPHY

The author is a former long-term banker by profession and worked within the Bank's Credit Card Fraud Team, where he obtained a Private Investigators Licence. The author resides between Adelaide, South Australia, and the Sunshine Coast, Queensland.

In November 2022, the author won an award from Wakefield Press, Adelaide for his short story: 'Car on a Hill'.